Hunt the Fat White Vampire

Andrew Fox

MonstraCity Press Manassas, Virginia

MonstraCity Press

MonstraCity Press

Manassas, Virginia

www.monstracitypress.com

ISBN-13: 978-1-954977-99-0

Books by Andrew Fox

FAT WHITE VAMPIRE SERIES

Fat White Vampire Blues (Del Rey Books)

Bride of the Fat White Vampire (Del Rey Books)

The Bad Luck Spirits' Social Aid and Pleasure Club (tie-in)

Fat White Vampire Otaku

Hunt the Fat White Vampire

The Good Humor Man, or, Calorie 3501 (Tachyon Publications)

THE AUGUST MICHOLSON CHRONICLES

Fire on Iron

Hellfire and Damnation (available August 2021)

COLLECTIONS

Hazardous Imaginings: The Mondo Book of Politically Incorrect Science Fiction

EDITED BY ANDREW FOX

Again, Hazardous Imaginings: More Politically Incorrect Science Fiction for Dara, who successfully hunted me down

One

JONATHAN of the High Krewe of Vlad Tepes belched. Loudly. It was a resonant belch, issuing from the pit of his stomach, redolent with the iron-tinged aftertaste so common to a large meal of blood. He licked his lips swiftly to catch that aftertaste before it faded. *Yum.*

It wasn't a gracious noise, or a diffident noise, especially not bursting forth from the mouth of one of the little princelings of the High Krewe. As was his habit, he had ensconced himself after his liquid dinner in the commodious living room of the High Krewe's mansion, a walled compound located near the western boundary of the city of New Orleans.

A belch, he knew, indicated satisfaction with a meal. And why not? His blood-meal was the most healthful to be found anywhere in New Orleans, courtesy of Straussman, the butler, who tended the herd of blood "cows" (actually mentally deficient humans) housed in a dormitory adjacent to this mansion within whose living room he loafed, while endlessly clicking through TV channels with the remote.

Yes, his belch signaled satisfaction, and it bespoke confidence in his status as princeling. And boredom with that status. Nothing remotely exciting had happened to him since the day a little over three years ago when that fat detective had freed him from the blood-thirsty clutches of Courane L'Enfant and his mistresses.

The TV failed to provide him with even a modicum of relief from his boredom. *Four hundred channels to flip through, and not a whiff of excitement,* he moaned to himself. *And the Saints can't avoid a losing season at this point, so none of the sports commentary channels are worth a moment of my precious time.* He returned to aimlessly pressing the up arrow on his remote, until the TV flashed through the highest channels in its range and returned to the lowest channels, those remote regions of public access television and amateur broadcasting.

One show caught his midnight blue eye. He twisted his fingers through his long, rich, blonde curls as he found himself watching it. It was called *The Morganna the Marvelous Show,* hosted, of course, by a woman who called herself Morganna the Marvelous. What she hosted was a series of older horror and science fiction movies which had fallen into the public domain. Tonight's installment was an old Japanese anime feature called *Matsuba, Shina Myoushu,* which roughly translated to *Matsuba, Matter Master.* It was about a Japanese superhero who made his headquarters in Tokyo.

Jonathan had never watched it before. It had a rough-edged charm. Its star's super-power was to control matter; he could mentally transform one form of matter into virtually any other form, limited only by his imagination. The production values were cheap. The animators had skimped on the number of cells they had drawn, and the film featured so few cells per second that the animated figures on the screen seemed to jerk from step to step, and of course the movement of their mouths never matched up with the (English language) words they spoke (maybe they matched up better when the characters were speaking in their original Japanese?). Still, Jonathan found the movie oddly watchable.

Then, during the couple of minutes which on a commercial station would be filled with televised ads, the hostess, Morganna the Marvelous, offered her commentary on the movie. "Do you think it *matters* to Matsuba that his film is so doggone awful? Or has he *mastered* the temptation to vomit every time he has to recite one of those dreadful lines of dialogue?" The studio audience groaned at the awkward puns on the film's title. "You think you can do any better?" Morganna asked, challenging her audience. "Okay, let's see who can do better! I'm going to randomly select two audience members to cast down to the Self-Abasement Basement until they can make their fellow audience members laugh. Here I go! I'm picking two numbers from the spinner, and if you have one of those picked numbers on the bottom of your chair, sir or madame, you are exiled to the Self-Abasement Basement until you manage to produce some laughter from this group!"

Damn it, I know her from somewhere. Jonathan thought something looked very familiar about Morganna the Marvelous, although he had never before watched her show. He somehow knew Morganna wasn't her real name, but her real name did start with the letter M. He called over his auburn-haired companion in the living room to sit beside him on the couch and stare at the screen. "Hey, Pearl! Come on over here and sit your shapely behind down next to me and see if you can figure out where we know this Morganna from. Don't we know her from somewhere?"

Pearl's heart-shaped face distorted with a frown of distress. She stood a good six inches taller than her rather diminutive companion. "Oh, Jonathan, haven't I told you never to *talk* when I'm here in the living room with you? Hearing your pre-pubescent voice raises hackles on the back of my neck. How I miss Randolph! He was even shorter than you, but at least he was a real man! He had class! He had *presence!*"

"Forget about 'Real-Man Randolph' for just a sec, okay? Come here and sit down and watch this with me. I'm sure I know this Morganna woman from somewhere, and I figure you must, too. Your mission, whether or not you choose to accept it, is to help me remember from where. Now, take a good look, and tell me how we know her..."

Pearl pushed her glasses (featuring rose-tinted, heart-shaped lenses mounted in a fire-engine red set of frames) up to the bridge of her nose and stared hard at the TV. Concentrating on the image, she chewed her wad of bubble gum with renewed enthusiasm. "Yes! Yes, we *do* know her! I know who that is! That's Maureen! She used to be one of us, almost a hundred years ago! Straussman the butler turned her and brought her into the High Krewe. But she didn't last here long. She went outside and worked as a singer in a saloon and turned a man who ended up becoming her lover — that dreadful fat detective who rescued you and me. You remember him, I'm sure? Jules Duchon?"

Jonathan's eyes didn't leave the screen. He suddenly clapped his ivory hands. "You know, it's not just her face that looks so darn familiar. It's her *legs,* too. Not that I'm a leg-man, but once you've seen legs like those, you never forget them. Take a look at those gams, Pearl — don't they look an awful lot like the pair which used to prop up our old friend Victoria?"

"Now that you mention it — *yes,* they do look *familiar!* Those muscles — Victoria always prided herself on her prowess as a dancer and an athlete! She used to put me down for spending so much of my time chewing bubble gum and watching so much TV, said I'd grow a heart-shaped *ass* to match my heart-shaped face if I didn't start getting regular exercise. Yeah, those fishnet stockings don't leave much to the imagination, even though the vampiress legs they're covering look invisible on the TV, 'cause vampire flesh can't be photographed. That pretty much makes it *certain* it's Maureen we're looking at, huh? I mean, which other white female vampires would be running around loose in New Orleans, hosting a public access TV show? Victoria, Alexandra, and Flora Ann used to go wandering, but none of them is in any shape to go no place anymore, and that dame on the TV sure isn't *me!* I mean, public access TV is *live* TV, right? Which means she's hosting that show right now? At five minutes to midnight?"

"Yeah, they don't tape these shows for later broadcast," Jonathan said. "It's live. What we're watching is actually going down in some crummy public access TV studio right now. Just one little problem, though. According to the fat detective, who should know, isn't Maureen *dead?* I mean, wasn't her death what made him change himself into two or three hundred white rats and hide out in the crawl spaces beneath buildings in the Quarter, until the Triumvirate convinced that cross-dressing character Rory 'Doodlebug' Richelieu to round up the rats and force them to transform themselves back into Jules Duchon?"

"Oh my gosh, *yes!* When you're right, you're right, Jonathan," Pearl said, growing more excited. "She was supposed to be dead as a rat whose neck got snapped by a trap. But Jonathan, I'd recognize that face anywhere, even all coated with makeup like it is! *And* those legs! Say, the fat detective never recovered Victoria's legs, did he? Nor Alexandra's arms, nor Flora Ann's torso. That's why those three gals all remain in comas, lying in their coffins stuck away in our biggest storage room."

Something else occurred to her. "Hey, that Doodlebug character was supposed to be a wiz with the old vampire spells, wasn't he? Do you think maybe it was possible he used some old spell to partially resurrect Maureen from the dead, and then he took just her head — stay with me here, Jonathan! — and he attached her head to Flora Ann's torso, then attached Flora Ann's torso to Alexandra's arms and Victoria's legs? So the Maureen we're seeing on TV now is actually a *Frankenstein* Maureen, made up of her own head and body parts from three different vampiresses? Doesn't that fat detective hang out with a medical doctor? Couldn't the medical doctor have sewn all those different parts together? Do you think I'm onto something here, Jonathan?"

"To steal a line from Abraham Lincoln, who quoted a little girl he knew who put her foot in her stocking — 'I think there's something in it.' Yeah, I think you're onto something, Pearl! Let me ask you, since you knew them better than I did, did Alexandra, Flora Ann, or Victoria have any distinguishing markings on their bodies? I mean, stuff that wouldn't show on the TV, like a tattoo or a birthmark? Stuff that we could look for and maybe spot in person if we found a way to get ourselves included in that studio audience?"

Pearl scrunched up her face. "Let me think, let me think... *yes!* Alexandra had a tattoo of a rose on her left biceps! Flora Ann had a little

Chinese dragon tattooed on her right breast, I'm sure of it. And I'm almost positive I remember that Victoria had a prominent mole on one of her inner thighs, that she used to try to cover up with makeup, but it was so sticky-outey, you couldn't help but see it anyway!"

"Now that you mention it — isn't that a *lump* on Morganna's inner left thigh? Couldn't that be a *mole?"*

"Good eyes, Jonathan! Even though you never officially passed through puberty, those little blue eyes of yours are as sharp as an eagle's! That's a big sticky-outey mole, for sure! So now I'm *positive* we're staring at Victoria's legs!"

"We've got to let Krauss, Katz, and Bestoff know what we've seen, Pearl."

"Oh, for *sure,* Jonathan! This will earn us *major* props with the Triumvirate! Those creepy old dudes have been moaning and whining about the loss of their oh-so-precious *'chil-drun'* for over three years now. They've sworn vengeance on whoever stole body parts from Alexandra, Victoria, and Flora Ann and cast those three girls into comas. I sure as heck wouldn't want to be in Maureen's dancing shoes now!"

"How did she do it, though, if she was dead at the time? I guess she must've had help, like you said? Maybe from that doctor dude the fat detective hangs with and from that cross-dressing vampire who knows spells?"

"We can let Krauss, Katz, and Bestoff sort it all out," Pearl said. "They insist they're the brains of the High Krewe, anyway, so let them do the heavy thinking. Hey, I've thought of something. Just by watching the show, we were able to verify that Maureen's legs once belonged to Victoria, because of Victoria's sticky-outey mole. But Alexandra's and Flora Ann's tattoos are flat on their skin, so they wouldn't protrude through clothing like Victoria's mole does. Those tattoos won't show up on TV, but we could spot them in person! If we could get ourselves included as part of that studio audience, we could verify for the Triumvirate that those arms and torso originally belonged to Alexandra and Flora Ann.

"Better still, I could figure out a way to trap Maureen and get her back here to the compound, where the Triumvirate could force her to surrender her stolen body parts! Talk about vengeance — all Maureen would be left with would be her head! Jonathan, do you know what you have to do to get yourself included as part of the audience for *The Morganna the Marvelous Show?*"

"Let's keep on watching," Jonathan said. "Maybe they'll do some kind of an announcement before they go back to showing the movie."

Not more than thirty seconds later, a printed announcement appeared on screen:

If you'd like to be a member of the studio audience for The Morganna the Marvelous Show, *it's easy! Just sign up to take the* Real *New Orleans Vampire Tour, and attendance at a live broadcast of* The Morganna the Marvelous Show *is included in the price of admission! Discounted tickets are available for those brave souls who are willing to donate blood to the vampire! For more information and to purchase tickets online, visit the Internet home of the* Real *New Orleans Vampire Tour at www.realneworleansvampiretour.com.*

"That seems easy enough," Jonathan said. "I'll bet that *Real* New Orleans Vampire Tour is a hoot, anyway. Between the tour and the broadcast, sounds like a whole evening of good, clean, family fun."

"There's just one thing you've got to promise me, Jonathan."

"Sure. What is it?"

"We'll tell the Triumvirate what we've just seen on TV, of course. But let's keep my plan for you and me to visit a broadcast of *The Morganna the Marvelous Show* to ourselves, okay? You know how twitchy Krauss, Bestoff, and Katz get about any of us venturing outside the compound, ever since Flora Ann, Victoria, and Alexandra got their body parts removed and you and I got kidnapped and Maxim and Randolph got disappeared. I don't want the Triumvirate to have a chance to put us on lock-down before we're able to get outside these walls and take that vampire tour, okay? But I'm sure that if we're able to capture Maureen and bring her back her for the Triumvirate to dismember, all will be forgiven, won't it?"

"Yeah, sure," Jonathan said. "You can't argue with success."

"So you agree that we'll keep my plan to ourselves?"

Jonathan pantomimed locking his lips with an oversized padlock and key. "Mum's the word, Pearl!"

Two

"JULES, are you *sure* it wouldn't be appropriate for me to go out with the family tonight to the Trolley Stop Café dressed in my Morganna the Marvelous get-up?"

"Mo, we been over this half a dozen times already," Jules said to his wife. He shifted the bulk of his imposing three-hundred-and-twenty-pound undead mass from the middle of the sofa to one of its ends, making a cluster of steel coils groan in a symphony of protest. This being a Monday night, it was the only night of the week when Jules' living room sofa wasn't surrounded by phlebotomy tables, all awaiting tour-goers who were willing to part with a pint of blood in exchange for a hefty discount on the price of *Real* New Orleans Vampire Tour tickets. "It's our night off from our jobs — don't you want to spend just one night of the week dressed in *normal* goin'-out clothes? Besides, the Trolley Stop ain't the kinda place where you wanna be puttin' on airs—"

"Since when did wearing my costume in public become 'puttin' on airs'?"

"Since you became a minor public access TV starlet, that's when. Look, most of the regular clientele at the Trolley Stop are ordinary cops, cabbies, and paramedics—"

"*They* all wear uniforms, don't they? So what would be the difference between them doing so and me wearing *mine?*"

"The difference is, hon, you'd be the only one there whose wearing of her uniform could be looked at as a desperate attempt to shout, '*Look at me! I'm that gal from TV!*' The difference is, none of the cops or cabbies or paramedics care anything about gettin' noticed or gettin' stared at."

"*I* don't care about getting noticed. I get noticed plenty enough as is, thanks to this fine, feline figure I filched from Alexandra, Victoria, and Flora Ann. Y'know, I hardly feel guilty anymore for walking around with their body parts, Jules. That trio of bitchy vampiresses would've filled my ears to overflowing with insults if they had known me during my 'person of size' phase. I'd offer daily hosannas of praise to my father in-law Doc Landrieu and to Doodlebug for piecing together this nifty replacement body for me, if only..."

"If only Alexandra, Victoria, and Flora Ann weren't physically repulsed by your husband and hadn't found a way to express that revulsion in ways that can't be ignored, huh?" Even though he knew the outcome of his effort, Jules reached for his wife's purloined arm to give it an affectionate squeeze. But before his fingers could get within six inches of Maureen's toned biceps, her arm flinched away from him, as though his fingertips had been charged with pain-inducing static electricity.

"Oh, Jules," Maureen moaned, "why do you even *try* anymore? What's changed tonight that would make my reaction to your attempt at a caress any different from my reaction any other night?"

"Nothin', absolutely nothin'. But the night I give up tryin' is the night I crawl back into my coffin and don't come out anymore. One of these nights, maybe Flora Ann, Victoria, and Alexandra'll finally get used to me."

"If only Doodlebug had been able to use his network of contacts in the zoology and marine biology fields to gather together all the exotic ingredients that Super-Genius Jules's antidote requires! The antidote to the side-effect Kenji the Bonsai Master's whoopy-fun blood has on me, the side-effect that gives consciousness to Alexandra's arms and Victoria's legs and Flora Ann's torso. I can't stand the fact that my various body parts now all have a *veto vote* in whether or not I can make love with my husband!"

"Awww, hon, don't get too worked up over that antidote thingie," Jules counseled (he wanted to pat her hand reassuringly, but he knew that would be a futile gesture, for more reasons than one). "For all we know, that super-asshole Super-Genius Jules shared that recipe with you as a gag, just to get your hopes up—"

"No! He was *sincere!* I could tell from his voice when he listed the ingredients for me! Nobody knows your moods and your tones of voice better than me, Jules Duchon! And accept it or not, Super-Genius Jules is made up of one-hundred-and-eighty pounds of *you,* thanks to that big chunk of mass he stole from you to make a separate body for himself before he skedaddled out to sea. He can't hide his emotions from me any better than *you* can, Jules. I know what I heard. Super-Genius Jules was one-hundred-percent *genuine.*"

"Well, I wasn't there, so I just have to take your word as to my big-headed twin's sincerity. Anyway, isn't this what you call a moot point? I mean, there ain't no way Doodlebug's gonna be able to pull together all them crazy, exotic ingredients — fresh venom from a dwarf sea snake and a blue-ringed octopus and what not — to make up your antidote, real or a gag. So what's the use of you and me arguin' over it? We got plenty of other stuff to argue about, don't we? Do we hafta go lookin' for moot points to argue about, too?"

"Oh, I suppose not," Maureen sighed.

"Good. 'Cause it's just about time we head over to pick up Doc and my mother. Doc said he'd meet us over at the Trolley Stop for eight, but I said I'd rather we all go together. The Caddy don't get too many opportunities for cruisin' around town now that I ain't usin' her as a cab no more. She needs her exercise. Unlike me — I do so much walkin' around the French Quarter nowadays, directin' my tours, I'm in danger of acquirin' a girlish figure." He poked his midsection, which, while considerably less flouncy than it had been before Super-Genius Jules made off with one-hundred-and-eighty of Jules' former five hundred pounds, still had a whole lot of flounce left in it.

"Oh, *that'll* be the day, Jules Duchon! You needn't worry about melting away to a slender little nothing, hubby mine. You know, Super-Genius Jules needn't have been so parsimonious when he decided how much mass to filch from you a few months back. Just one-hundred-and-eighty pounds? He could've stolen *two-hundred-and-eighty* pounds instead and still left my husband a monument of a man."

"Be careful who you're callin' a *monument,* babe—"

"Oh, Jules, that was meant to be a *compliment!*"

"Yeah? Well, it depends. I mean, you've got the Washington Monument, which is all tall and slender and graceful-lookin', and then you got Mount Rushmore, which is, y'know, a dumpy ol' mountain with four faces carved into it."

"So think of yourself as the Washington Monument, hon, if that makes you feel better."

"Y'know, wasn't all that long ago that you could've called *yourself* a monument," Jules added. "In the good ol' days right after you took a toot of Emiko's mutant blood, you'd swelled up to about a quarter of the size of our bedroom, thanks to her blood grabbin' hold of that nightmare you'd been havin', that bad dream about you gainin' all your old weight back, and the blood usin' it as a template for what to change you into. Hey, I wouldn't mind it so much if we *both* took another swig of Emiko's blood, and you changed back into your eight-hundred-pound fatty self and I changed back into a big, horny, white rabbit. At least Alexandra's arms and Victoria's legs and Flora Ann's torso didn't seem to mind me at all when I had giant rabbit's feet and cuddly fur. That was the last time we got any good lovin' done. We'd just hafta avoid Shogo's blood this time, the mutant blood that turned me from a nice rabbit into a nasty rabbit."

Maureen frowned. "Even if we had a whole Thermos full of Emiko's mutant blood right here in front of us, I doubt it would work that way, Jules. I haven't been having my nightmares about gaining my old weight back recently, so those mental images aren't at the top of my mind. And you haven't had that spoiled little boy wearing the Disney *Alice in Wonderland* White Rabbit shirt take your tour in months, so the image from his shirt isn't at the top of *your* mind, either—"

"Yeah, I guess if I drank a big swig of Emiko's blood right now, I'd have as much chance of turnin' back into some version of big-head Super-Genius Jules again as I would into a big, horny, white rabbit, huh?"

"And having just one example of Super-Genius Jules slouching around somewhere in the vicinity of New Orleans is more than enough. We don't need *two*."

"Amen to that, babe," Jules said, nodding avidly. "Spendin' just a couple of hours as that giant-headed asshole was more than enough for me. I don't need a second trip on that E-ticket ride."

"Although if he split off from you *again* and took a second hundred-and-eighty pounds with him, he'd leave you with only a hundred and forty pounds, hon. You'd be even thinner than you were when I first put the bite on you back in 1917..."

"Didn't you just tell me my skinny days are over and done with? Whadda you want to turn me into a wrung-out dish rag for, anyway? You think that'd make Alexandra, Flora Ann, and Victoria any happier with me?"

"Oh, you know *I* don't mind you big and corpulent, Jules. But those three? I think their tastes in men run more towards Johnny Depp than Orson Welles, dear."

"Well, they're just gonna hafta get used to me the way I am, sooner or later," Jules huffed. "If they ever wanna get themselves any lovin' ever again, that is. Now, c'mon — let's go pick up your in-laws and head on over to the Trolley Stop before the joint runs outta omelets."

"Oh, Amos," Edna Landrieu purred prettily to her husband in the back seat of Jules' Cadillac Sedan de Ville, "do you think it would be all right if I ordered the steak and eggs tonight?"

Out of old habit acquired from years and years of *schlepping* around human fares in the back seat of his Caddy, Jules glanced quickly in his rear-view mirror to catch his step-father's expression. All he saw was Amos's hat shift uneasily on top of an invisible-to-the-mirror head. But he didn't have to see Amos's expression to imagine the consternation on his mother's husband's face. "Edna, my dearest darling," his step-father sputtered, "I really don't think your ordering a juicy slab of beef would be a good choice, this evening or any other— "

"Mom," Jules interjected, still looking in the rear-view mirror (he could see his mother's hair, thanks to the purple dye it had been infused with), "what Amos means to say, but he's too polite to tell you straight out, is there's too much chance of you insisting on that steak bein' cooked rare and bloody. Stick to a cheese omelet, okay? I'm sure you remember what happened the last time you dipped your fangs into some blood— "

"Now, Jules Augustine Duchon, you know very well I got turned into an old-lady-shaped vampire vacuum cleaner the last time I took me a good swig of blood. But it wasn't my fault, baby boy! I got tricked by that Shogo character into drinking a mix of his blood and his cousin Emiko's. Since I'd been spendin' all my time day-dreamin' about that super new vacuum cleaner I wanted Amos to buy for me, I ended up with vacuum cleaner nozzles for hands and hoses for arms, with a bad attitude to match. Can't you get it through your thick skull that there's a big difference between me eating' meat containin' a tablespoon or two of *cow's blood* and me gulpin' down a pint or so of *Japanese mutant superhero blood?* Ain't the same thing by a long shot, baby boy!"

"I completely agree, dearest," Amos said (Jules thought he overheard the sound of Amos's hand patting Edna's, although he couldn't be absolutely sure of it). "But what we want to all avoid is having you get used to the *taste* of blood, having you get used to the way blood *smells.* We wouldn't want the stuff to start appealing to you even *more* than it presently does..."

"But Amos, that cheddar cheese in diner omelets gets stuck between my teeth, and so do the seeds in the rye toast I end up ordering it with— "

"We'll stop off at the Rite-Aid for some dental floss on the way home," Jules offered. "That okay by you, Mom?"

"Oh, I suppose it'll have to do," Edna huffed. "You men — gangin' up on me to control what I put into my mouth! There oughta be a law against it!" Looking in his rear-view mirror, Jules saw the sleeves of his mother's sweater cross themselves beneath her bosom in an agitated fashion.

Jules chanced into a lucky parking place directly in front of the Trolley Stop Café's handicapped access ramp. Only after he turned off his ignition did he notice that he'd parked one spot distant from his old friend Erato's Lincoln Town Car taxi cab. *So Erato's takin' his early evening dinner break,* Jules thought. *And here I am, showin' up with my entire family in tow. Maybe seein' me steppin' up as a generous family man, takin' the old lady and the wife and the step-father out for a nice dinner, will unclog Erato's heart, and he'll acknowledge me when I say hello? It'd be the first time since my wedding that he'd have said word one to me.*

With a big flourish, Jules opened the café's front door for his wife, his mother, and Amos, hoping that his former best friend might notice his gallantry and quietly approve. *Erato's a good Christian man,* Jules thought. *Maybe he'll appreciate a show of good Christian manners, even from a vampire.*

Walking inside, Jules noticed that Erato was sitting at the counter with other cabbies and a few cops. Only one stool was still available, the one at the very end, next to where Erato was sitting. *If I were on my own, that's where I'd plop myself down,* Jules thought. *I always liked that end stool, 'cause it left me more space on my right side to let my belly hang out. But even if there were four stools sittin' empty, it would still be better for me to sit the family down at a proper table, where we can look at each other. Doc wouldn't like sittin' there at the counter with that big mirror starin' back at him from the far side of the bar, anyway; it would make him too nervous that somebody would notice that him and his missus don't cast no reflections. When I used to sit at the counter, I just said "heck with it" and let anybody who noticed my lack of reflection think whatever it was they was gonna think — like there was somethin' wrong with that portion of the mirror or somethin'. Didn't used to bother me much, what other people might think. And now that I'm headin' up the* Real *New Orleans Vampire Tour and I'm* supposed *to be a vampire, even a make-believe vampire, I care even less what other people might be thinkin'.*

Monday night wasn't a crowded night at the Trolley Stop, not like a Friday or Saturday night, so a waitress sat Jules's party at a table immediately. Amos ordered for both Edna and himself; a cheese omelet for her, a cheese and mushroom omelet for himself. Maureen ordered a green salad (*still watchin' her figure,* Jules grumbled to himself). Jules was the only one to not order any solid food (unlike the other vampires at the table, whose systems, for varying reasons, could still tolerate solid foods, he would have to transform himself into his wolf form in order to enjoy something like a cheese omelet, and ever since Super-Genius Jules had made off with one-hundred-and-eighty pounds of his mass, his accustomed vampire tricks had been out of his reach). He ordered his usual — black chicory coffee, telling the waitress to keep it coming.

He noticed his mother was staring avidly at Erato, and that Jules's former best friend was staring just as avidly at her. Edna reached across the table to poke her son. "Say, Jules, see that colored man over there at the counter, the sort of pudgy one with the lazy eye? Haven't I seen him before? I could swear he showed up at that joint wedding of ours, drunk as a skunk— "

"That's my old buddy Erato, Mom," Jules whispered back to her. "I asked him to be my best man at the wedding. He showed up late, just before the ceremony started, but he made it."

"Yes, *yes!* I remember him now! You passed him the wedding ring so he could hold it for you and pass it back to you to stick on Maureen's finger. Then, after the ceremony, he slunk off into a corner and stayed by himself, not sayin' a word to nobody, till you had that other friend of yours drive him home."

"Your memory's pretty good, Mom." Jules noticed that Erato was now awkwardly staring at both him and his mother. He offered his one-time closest human friend a comradely wave. "Hey, Erato! Good to see you! I kinda forgot this is your usual time for a mid-evening dinner break. See you're still keepin' that Lincoln of yours nicely waxed."

As soon as Jules waved, Erato swiveled on his stool back around toward the counter and his plate, turning his back on the corpulent vampire. Jules saw that Maureen had observed the entire transaction. "Jules, let me help you," she whispered to him.

"Huh? How you gonna help if Erato's insistin' on bein' obstinate about not acknowledgin' no vampires?"

"Jules Duchon, sometimes you don't know shit from shinola. In a situation like this, a little sugar is called for, don't you think? Erato doesn't have anything against me— "

"Aside from the fact that you're a blood-sucker and now he knows it and you offend his Christian beliefs."

"Well, yes, I mean aside from *that*. Didn't you tell me he volunteered to watch over my ashes while I was stuck in the netherworld after Malice X rammed a wooden stake through me?"

"Yeah, he did that for me. But that was before I was forced to admit to him I'm a vampire."

"And didn't he stand up for you as your best man the night when you married me?"

"Yeah, he did that for me, too."

"And that was *after* he knew you were a vampire. Well, then I figure he must have a soft spot in that heart of his where I'm concerned. Give me one of those free passes for the vampire tour that you carry around in your wallet."

"What you gonna do with it? Use it to stir his coffee for him?"

"*No,* dummy!" Maureen swatted him on his shoulder. "I'm going to invite him to take a complimentary tour and then join me at a broadcast of *The Morganna the Marvelous Show*. I'm going to explain to him that you're a legitimate businessman now, and you no longer find it necessary to put the bite on fares' necks. So are you gonna give me that pass, or not?"

Jules pulled his wallet out of his sport coat's pocket and handed her one of the free passes. "Okay," he said, "if you succeed in gettin' him to agree to go on our tour, your meal's on me."

"Oh, Jules!" she said, playfully swatting him again. "You were going to pay for my meal in any case. Now, watch a master at work and see how things get done."

She rose from her seat and sashayed over to Erato's place at the counter. "Good evening, Erato," she said after lightly touching him on his shoulder. "I'm not certain you'd remember me. I'm Maureen Duchon."

Erato, flinching slightly at her touch, looked up at her. "Oh, I remember who you are, Mrs. Duchon."

"Please, call me Maureen. We're all friends here."

"If you say so, Maureen."

"Good, that's better. Now, let me tell you one thing before saying anything else. Jules did not send me over here to talk to you. It was *my* idea. Jules was afraid of disturbing your dinner hour, but I'm not so prissy about such niceties. If you don't mind my saying so, I noticed that you looked away when my husband tried catching your attention with a friendly greeting just now. Again, if you don't mind my saying so, that hurt his feelings. A lot. As Jules's loving wife, I don't appreciate it when someone hurts my husband's feelings. You and Jules were best friends for years. He asked you to be his best man at his wedding. Is there a reason you won't talk to him now?"

Erato blanched. "He's... if you don't mind my saying so, Maureen, Jules is, well, he's a *murderer*. Worse, an *unrepentant* murderer. It goes against my Christian beliefs to associate with a person like that."

"Well, then I'd say you're a little behind the times, Erato," Maureen said. "Jules would like you to know that he no longer captures fares in his cab and drinks their blood until they are dead. In fact, he no longer utilizes his Cadillac as a cab-for-hire. All that changed after Hurricane Antonia blew through town. The storm really dried up the taxi cab business for a while— "

"Oh, yes, I remember that oh-too-well."

"Jules found himself without customers. So he decided to try out something else. With the help of the Small Business Administration and FEMA, who gave him a loan on good terms, he started a small business called the *Real* New Orleans Vampire Tour. You being in the hospitality business yourself, maybe you've heard of it?"

Erato nodded, his lazy eye straying to the mirror where Maureen's reflection failed to show. "Yes, ma'am, I've heard talk of it."

"Have you heard of the special discounts the tour offers to any customers who volunteer to donate blood?"

"Yes, ma'am, I've had a few fares mention that. They think it's mighty peculiar, but strangely appealing."

"Well, that's real good to hear," Maureen said. "See, those blood donations from willing volunteers are filling in for the blood Jules used to extract from victims in his cab. Also, he's got his mother Edna over there, her husband Amos sitting across from her, and me all helping out with the business. Edna sells souvenirs, Amos does the phlebotomy work, and I act as horror hostess for a nightly public access TV sci-fi and monster movie show; we all take a break on Monday nights, and Jules decided to treat everyone for dinner tonight as a thank-you for all the good work we've been doing for the business. Jules is very proud of the fact that he's set things up in such a way that not one, not two, but *four* New Orleans blood-drinkers are taken off the hunt. Don't you think that's a major accomplishment?"

Erato considered this for a moment. Finally, he nodded. "Uh, yes, ma'am. I'd have to admit, that's a big step forward out of the darkness. Nobody with a Christian heart could deny that fact."

"Well, there you go." She placed the free tour pass down on the counter next to Erato's butter knife. "Here's a little something for you. Jules and I would like to invite you to attend one of our vampire tours and the broadcast of one of my shows, free of charge. This pass is good for any night, aside from a Monday, that you'd like to use it for. The tour is very educational and amusing, and I always manage to pick out one of those 'so-bad-it's-good' sci-fi or monster movies to poke fun at on my show. It's a hoot. Can Jules and I count on you to make use of this free pass sometime soon? We'd sure like to show you in person how we've all made that big step forward out of the darkness and become good corporate citizens of New Orleans." She smiled, briefly flashing her dainty fangs.

Erato picked up the pass and held it so that he could take a close look at it. "Sure thing, Maureen. I usually take a night off from driving my hack on Thursdays. One of these Thursdays coming up, I'll be sure to pay you all a visit. And I thank you... and Jules."

"That's what I wanted to hear, Erato. Thanks!" She gave him a light peck on his cheek before heading back to her table. She winked at her husband, who'd been watching the whole interaction, before she sat back down. "Now you see how business gets done. You've got to use a little sugar, sugar!"

Three

THREE vampires of vastly differing stature but of equal rank sat on plush chairs around a conference table within the library of the High Krewe of Vlad Tepes and pondered on what one of the junior members of their association, Jonathan Preston, had just revealed.

The member of the Triumvirate who appeared to be by far the oldest (although he was only a century older than either of his colleagues in undead years), Nikolas Katz, interlocked his liver-spotted talons beneath his eggplant-shaped chin and peered over at Georges Besthoff. Besthoff was the High Krewe potentate who served as the "public face" of the Triumvirate and who most often dealt in face-to-face matters with the compound's staff of servants and with the junior vampires. "Georges," he said, his voice a rambling cackle which sounded a lot like Bela Lugosi on a sterno bender, "did the yunk miss-uzz, Pearl, have anythink to say to you that the yunk master, Jonathan, did not just report?" As a quiet afterthought, he added, almost as if speaking to himself, "I *like* that Jonathan. He is... succulent and tast-tee, hee-hee!"

Georges Besthoff cleared his throat with distinct discomfort. Now that there were so many fewer junior vampires (*de chil-drun,* as Katz referred to them, hungrily) active within the compound — Maxim and Randolph had been missing these past few years and were presumed deceased, and Victoria, Alexandra, and Flora Ann were all trapped in a comatose state, confined to their coffins — his colleague Katz found himself with far fewer opportunities to indulge in his "rejuvenation evenings" with the youngsters. After all, there were only so many diddlings Jonathan and the pitifully few other boy vampires could be expected to endure, and even Pearl and her remaining young sisters became fatigued with too much of Katz's attentions. So the elderly vampire, more often than not, was stuck in his dilapidated septuagenarian's form, as he was tonight, denied his periodic and increasingly rare restorations to his more youthful state, which he now saved for "special occasions" only (like his deathday).

Gregory Krauss, the Triumvirate's third member, had exactly the opposite problem as Katz. He had been turned in the Old Country by a distinguished senior vampire when he was twelve years old, just before he would have entered into puberty. So when he was forced to interact with the staff or with the compound's junior vampires, as he had been tonight, he invariably took the time to apply silver powder to his long sideburns and the hair above his slightly pointed ears, so that his appearance could at least somewhat match the seniority and dignity of his long span of undead years.

I'm the only one of us three who never has to concern himself with disguising or altering my age, Georges Besthoff thought. *I suppose that makes me the most fortunate of us three.*

"Well, Georges," Krauss said in his gratingly high-pitch pre-pubescent voice, which no amount of silver hair makeup could disguise, "I haven't heard an answer from you to Nikolas's question. I was wondering the same thing, myself. Did Pearl reveal anything to you which Jonathan failed to comment upon just now?"

"No. Jonathan was quite complete in his reportage of what the two of them discovered by watching television. I can only assume that our former protégé Maureen Remoulade has become... rather less discreet in her dealings with mortals since she inhabited our compound here, nearly a century past."

"Maureen Remoulade..." Katz scowled as he brought to mind the dim memory of one of the few among the High Krewe's young vampires who had escaped his embraces. "She vas that leetle blonde, vas she not? The von vhich Straussman turned to our way, the von vhich Straussman, our own servant, vould never allow me to breeng into my bed?"

"Yes, Nikolas, we've gone over this multiple times," the boyish Krauss sighed (*when he sighs, Gregory's voice is indistinguishable from an adult woman's,* Besthoff mentally noted). "Straussman threatened to quit on us if you ever placed an errant hand upon the girl he intended for his bride. He was such a good butler, we didn't want to risk losing him, so we decided, as a Triumvirate, that you would steer clear of her. Although it appears that his protestations on her behalf backfired rather badly, being as how she ended up consorting first with Jules Duchon and later with that Negro Malice X, whom she, to her own eventual sorrow, turned to vampirism."

"Still," Besthoff said, "I believe that Straussman, despite all his years of service to us and his declarations of undying loyalty to the High Krewe, is the key to this seeming mystery which Jonathan has brought to our attention. I believe the attacks on our members could not have been accomplished so efficiently without the aid of an inside man, someone within our house who could inform an outside assailant whenever one of our young members would leave the safety of our compound and head to the bowels of the city in search of prey or profit (we know not which). And who among us but Straussman, the vampire who turned her, would retain vestigial ties of affection to Maureen Remoulade and desire her resurrection from the limbo of non-existence?"

Krauss smoothed his "frosted" sideburns away from his cheeks, leaving traces of silver makeup on his fingertips. "Georges," he said slowly, "I must say I agree with your analysis of the situation, such as it is. However, entirely apart from what I am sure will be Straussman's impassioned protestations of innocence in this matter, there are his undoubtable skills as a veteran vampire which we must take into account; we would not want to make an enemy of such a personage without good cause. Our experience with the obese and proletarian Jules Duchon, whom we attempted to manipulate to our own ends some years ago, has shown us that even a vampire of low cunning is not a creature to be taken lightly. You propose that we level a charge of high treason against our oldest servant, whose loyalty is of many centuries standing. I am sure I speak for Nikolas, as well, when I state I would not agree to any moves against this upstanding servant without some form of proof of his perfidy — Nikolas, you are free, of course, to disagree with what I have just said."

The dilapidated vampire waved away any notion that he might disagree with his junior colleague on this, fanning one of his talons in front of his hooked nose as though he were trying to dismiss a bad odor or discourage flies from landing there. "No, no, no, no, *no* — I fully *agree,* Gregory!"

"So how do you plan to collect such proof, Georges?" Krauss continued. "You cannot fail to recollect that you, yourself, chose to turn Straussman back in the Old Country. He is your blood-son. And in terms of centuries as a vampire, he is not so much junior to you or to me, despite his lowly status among us."

"This is what I propose," Besthoff announced. He had been mulling over this plan in his head ever since Jonathan had shared the news of his most likely having spotted Maureen Remoulade hosting a television program absurdly titled *The Morganna the Marvelous Show.* "If we three are in agreement with this, let us alert Straussman this evening as to his blood-daughter's reappearance. Let us then place his communications under close surveillance. Otranto or Hecht, Straussman's fellow man servants, can electronically listen in on any telephone conversations which Straussman initiates from our compound. Should he attempt to leave the compound, possibly to alert his co-conspirators in this matter, I propose we should have him followed."

"By 'co-conspirators in this matter,'" Krauss said, "may I assume you mean our former stooge Jules Duchon and perhaps some of his other confederates?"

"That is my expectation, unfortunately, yes."

"Then I must say I agree with this plan. Nikolas, what is your say in the matter?"

"Oh, I *like* thees plan!" the elderly vampire cackled. "Eef eet will bring me back de chil-drun who now sleep in their coffins so that they may keep me company in my bed, I like thees plan very much!"

Besthoff kept his steely gray eyes affixed on Straussman's pale, sallow face as the tall, ramrod-straight butler stood at attention next to the library table and faced his three masters. How odd that Gregory should have mentioned tonight the fact that the butler had originally joined the High Krewe as one of Besthoff's many blood-children. Besthoff had spent so many decades interacting with him as a man servant, he had temporarily forgotten there was ever any familial connection between them. How doubly odd, then, that of the three of them, Besthoff, the butler's blood-father, should have been the one to direct the finger of blame at Straussman. *Fate often works in strange ways,* Besthoff mused silently.

"Yes, masters?" Straussman said in an even tone of voice. "Otranto informed me that my presence is required. How may I serve my masters this evening, apart from my normal duties?"

"This does not pertain to any additional duties, Straussman," Besthoff said. "My fellow rulers and I have news to share with you. Two of our junior members discovered this evening that your blood-daughter, Maureen Remoulade, has returned from the netherworld."

Besthoff watched the butler slowly swallow, then brush his fingertips across his forehead. Such gestures could be signs of subdued surprise, or they could be the involuntary signifiers of... guilt.

Besthoff asked himself which he would prefer. The former would mean his blood-child's innocence, but it would also throw a road block across a promising avenue of investigation into the mystery of the current whereabouts of Alexandra's, Victoria's, and Flora Ann's missing body parts; the latter would mean that Besthoff and his two equals would have no recourse but to eliminate Straussman in some yet undetermined fashion. Besthoff decided he preferred the former; wholly apart from their familial connection, Straussman had been an excellent man servant and would prove enormously difficult to replace.

"For-forgive my momentary incoherence, masters," Straussman stuttered. "This comes as a tremendous surprise. A welcome surprise, surely, but an unsettling one. No vampire returns from the netherworld after being banished there as thoroughly as my blood-daughter was without... significant efforts having been undertaken on her behalf. Am I at liberty to ask who among us witnessed Maureen's return, and in what setting was she seen?"

"Those are acceptable and expected questions," Besthoff said. "Jonathan and Pearl were the ones who made the discovery. Earlier this evening Jonathan was in the den, scanning the television for programs of interest. He stumbled across one of most definite interest, a public access program entitled *The Morganna the Marvelous Show*. Pearl, who remembers Maureen well from Maureen's time here in the compound with us, recognized her former home-mate on the broadcast."

"But how is that possible, master?" Straussman asked. "The faces of our kind do not appear in photographs and are invisible in television broadcasts."

"Apparently Maureen made it possible for her visage to be broadcast over the airwaves by wearing full facial makeup and contact lenses, as well as a wig."

"So it is possible that Pearl could have been mistaken in her identification of Maureen, given all that effort at concealment by the person being broadcast?"

"It is possible, yes. But it is not very likely that Pearl would have been mistaken. Even covered with a thick coat of makeup, Miss Remoulade's features are quite distinctive, I am told. Was that not one of the main reasons you selected her as your consort-in-waiting, before she abandoned these walls forever?"

"I must admit that Maureen's striking facial features and beautiful blond hair were among the factors I considered when I chose her as my blood-daughter," Straussman said. "So I agree with your conclusion that Pearl was correct when she identified Maureen on the television program. But — but Maureen's return is so inexplicable... how could she have managed to return from the netherworld after having been reduced entirely to a pile of dust by her assailant, the Negro vampire Malice X? I am told she was not simply staked through the heart and her skeleton left with the wooden protuberance still poking through her rib cage; I was informed her death was far more thorough than this, so any resurrection would have required the services of a vampire well practiced in the mystical arts, not the mere removal of a wooden stake."

If Straussman was indeed guilty of some connection with his blood-daughter's mysterious resurrection, he is playing this well, Besthoff thought. "Do you intend to make any effort to contact her?"

The butler slowly shook his head. "No, masters," he said. "Maureen and I have not been in communication for many decades now. The last time we spoke was the year of America's entry into the First World War, more than a century ago. I — I would not know what to say to her at this point, apart from asking her how this miraculous resurrection of hers was accomplished."

A fine bit of misdirection you just threw in our paths, if indeed you are less than innocent. "That may be something which we will ask you to do at some point," Besthoff said. He decided it was best not to mention tonight a word of Pearl's suspicions that Maureen's resurrection was abetted by a pilferage of Alexandra's, Victoria's, and Flora Ann's missing body parts. All would hinge on how Straussman acted over the coming nights. "But we will not ask you this evening to attempt to reopen communications with your former paramour, Straussman. We merely thought it best to inform you of her mysterious reappearance. You are dismissed. Please return to your regular duties."

The three members of the Triumvirate waited until Straussman had exited the library before they resumed speaking with one another. "Well, Nikolas, Georges?" Krauss said. "What do you make of his reaction?"

"Ambiguous," Besthoff replied. "I will instruct Otranto and Hecht to immediately begin recording all telephonic communications which originate in our compound. I will also ensure that they utilize the tracking mechanisms which we have had installed in our fleet of automobiles, should Straussman make any move to leave our facilities."

Straussman located Besthoff in the latter's office early the following evening. "Master," the butler said, "I regret to inform you that I have been rather remiss in one of my duties. I have failed to keep a proper accounting of a vital portion of our provisions, and we have run short."

Besthoff stiffened slightly. This could be a prelude to a request by Straussman that he be allowed to utilize one of the compound's vehicles and travel off-site. "What is it that we are out of, Straussman?"

"Sanitary diapers for the herd. We simply cannot do without those, master. Should we run completely out, we risk the spread of disease among the imbeciles from whom we draw blood; should an appreciable number of the imbeciles fall ill, we will have suffered a degradation of our own food supply. Apparently, our provisioning company was temporarily out of this particular item when their delivery truck most recently visited us, and I was not properly informed. I request permission to take one of our station wagon vehicles into town to an all-night store such as GoodiesMart so that I may procure an emergency supply."

Whether he did so purposefully or not, Straussman had selected a time when both Otranto and Hecht were occupied with other duties in the compound; Besthoff doubted that, should he grant permission for Straussman to use a vehicle, he would have time to pull either of the other servants aside and get them into a second vehicle in time to tail Straussman. It appeared he would need to follow the butler himself.

"It is regrettable that this has happened, but I am glad you noticed our lack of an adequate supply before we completely ran out of sanitary diapers," Besthoff said. "I grant you permission to take one of the station wagons to the store. Just sign it out according to ordinary procedures."

"Thank you, master. I will go immediately."

Which of the other vehicles shall I take? Besthoff asked himself as the butler exited Besthoff's office. He wasn't certain that the compound's Audi TT sports coupe had been equipped with a GPS tracking device which would allow him to follow Straussman's wagon at a discrete distance. A safer bet would be to take one of the sedans. A dark four-door would blend in better with traffic than a bright-red sports coupe, in any case, Besthoff reminded himself.

He waited a moment after Straussman left the room, then rose from his desk. He hadn't had an opportunity to drive himself somewhere for a number of months. When he needed to go into the city, he generally had Straussman chauffeur him in one of the large sedans; the only times he drove himself were for pleasure, when he would take the sporty Audi coupe out for an occasional nighttime joy ride on some of the back roads on the West Bank of the Mississippi River. It would be a refreshing change of pace to drive himself. He might even have the opportunity to change himself into one of his other forms in the process of observing Straussman's movements and conversations. That, too, would be refreshing. *Assuming I am able to determine Straussman to be innocent...*

He paused by the interior door of the garage until he heard Straussman back the compound's BMW 5 Series station wagon out of the space and the garage's overhead door automatically close once the wagon had departed. Then he selected another of the compound's BMWs, the 7 Series sedan, to be his personal transportation for the evening.

He switched on the sedan's GPS tracking system and adjusted its sensitivity. Luckily, just the previous night he had spent some time familiarizing himself with the system so that he could better explain its functions to Hecht and Otranto; its operation was still fresh in his mind. The local street grid appeared on the eight-inch screen. He noticed a moving red light which indicated Straussman had just turned onto Metairie Road and headed east into the city. A stationary green light representing his own vehicle showed that Besthoff's BMW had not yet exited the garage. That would change momentarily.

He remotely opened the compound's front gate and drove out onto the long driveway which led through a small forest to Metairie Road. Using the GPS system proved even easier than Besthoff had anticipated. The car's own electronic voice told him when and where to turn to follow Straussman's path; if he didn't wish to, he need never gaze at the GPS screen to plot out his route. The central question in his mind should resolve itself soon: would Straussman head for a GoodiesMart store, as he had told Besthoff he would, or would he head for the home of Maureen Remoulade, or possibly that of Jules Duchon?

Besthoff had his answer soon enough. Straussman drove up the entrance ramp onto the Pontchartrain Expressway, but he did not subsequently take any of the exits which would lead either to the West Bank suburbs, where he could choose from several GoodiesMart stores, or the Lower Garden District, where another GoodiesMart store was located. Instead, he took the exit which would lead him into the French Quarter.

There are no GoodiesMarts or large, suburban-style stores of any kind in the French Quarter, Besthoff told himself. The weight of evidence was quickly swinging against the notion of Straussman's innocence.

The butler parked his station wagon in front of one of the French Quarter's multi-level townhouses. *That is not the site of a wholesale establishment or of a retail outlet of any sort; it is a private dwelling.*

Besthoff experienced a leadenness in the pit of his stomach; he truly had not wanted to believe a servant of such long standing could be so grievously disloyal as to conspire against members of his own household.

After pausing half a moment to ascertain which of the neighboring townhouses the butler would enter, shielded from Straussman's sight by tinted glass, Besthoff circled the block and found a parking spot on the opposite side.

"The best way to enter that dwelling, and to see with whom Straussman converses and listen in on that conversation, would be to do so as a rodent," Besthoff told himself. "As a rather small rat, one which can easily squeeze itself through tiny openings, imperfections in walls and windows."

He removed his clothes and placed them on the passenger seat beside him. He found that the notion of transforming himself into a rat made his skin tingle. He hadn't done this sort of thing, especially not for a purpose such as this one, in decades; but constant practice on transformations within the compound's gymnasium had kept his skills sharp nonetheless.

The only potential downside of his utilizing this method of surveillance of his errant man servant would be that it would require him to leave the door of his BMW slightly ajar, so that he could return to its cabin and redress himself in his clothes once he was done (as a rat, he would be unable to open the sedan's door). In this neighborhood — actually, in most any neighborhood of New Orleans nowadays, he mused — the danger existed that a thief would take advantage of a slightly opened door to make off with the vehicle. *That is a danger to which I will simply have to resign myself,* he told himself. *At the worst, I will spend a long evening scurrying back home to the compound or seeking shelter here, amongst the buried basements of the French Quarter's ancient buildings. It cannot be helped at this point, not if I wish to ascertain Straussman's purpose in coming to this place. The only alternative would be to perform my transformation outside of the car, on the sidewalk, in open sight of any passers-by; and that would not be prudent in the least.*

Now fully naked, he willed the greater portion of his bodily mass to travel through the frigid realm of null space, that mystic dimension so essential to all vampiric bodily transformations, and to take up residence as proto-matter in the bottom of his coffin. His form wavered, then shimmered, then seemed to mostly melt away as the great majority of his mass fled, to end up in the base of his coffin as a gray, jelly-like semi-liquid.

The mass which was left behind was comparably minute. It resolved itself into a gray roof rat. His newly sensitive nostrils filled with the scent of tanned leather seats as his whiskers wiggled. *I tend to forget how pleasurable it can be to have certain of one's senses so wildly extended when in animal form,* Besthoff briefly marveled. Then he crept through the narrow opening he had left between the BMW's door's edge and its sill and scampered down onto the sidewalk, still slightly suffused with the warmth remaining from the baking the sun had granted these concrete slabs during the daytime.

His legs, short but powerfully muscular, abetted by the superior traction provided by sharp claws, allowed him to circle the block in the space of but a moment. Recalling which townhome Straussman had entered, Besthoff ran his front claws along the wooden frames of each window on the lowest level until he located one with part of its weather-stripping broken off. It was a tight squeeze, but with focused effort he managed to shimmy his way through the gap and enter the dimly lit abode.

He did not need to scamper across many rooms before he heard Straussman's voice coming from the next room over. He inserted himself into the room from which he smelled vampiric scents emanating, that sickly-sweet mixture of earth from the base of a coffin and dry, almost bloodless flesh which came across so pungently to the sensitive nose of a rodent.

He saw his butler standing in a parlor of some sort, a room crowded with chairs and with odd, padded tables such as might be seen in a physician's office. He also saw the grossly corpulent vampire, Jules Duchon, standing next to a blond vampiress who, from the descriptions provided by Pearl and Jonathan, Besthoff could only assume to be the mysteriously returned Maureen Remoulade. The trio was accompanied by a fourth person, who also smelled like a vampire, although Besthoff had no notion who this person was. The small rat hid in the shadows alongside the wall.

"Thank you all for seeing me," Straussman said.

"What, did you think we was gonna leave you hangin' at our front door?" Jules said. "It's not like you make it a habit of regularly payin' us social calls, Straussman."

"Jules is right, Johann," the woman whom Besthoff suspected to be Maureen Remoulade added. "We see you so rarely — this must be important. I know that Jules went to visit you in the immediate aftermath of Hurricane Antonia, but I hadn't seen you since you attended our wedding."

'Our wedding'? Besthoff thought in the darkness by the wall. *So the corpulent vampire and Maureen Remoulade are now married? When did this event take place, I wonder?*

"Yes, this is indeed important — I must bring a matter of *extreme* importance to your attention, I regret," Straussman told them. "The Triumvirate have been informed of Maureen's return to this plane of existence."

"How the heck did those three lame-ohs find out my wife was back in the flesh?" Jules said.

Besthoff's fur bristled at the notion that the obese, pitiably ill-educated vampire should cast aspersions upon him and his partners, all of whom vastly exceeded the cab-driving former detective in breeding and elocution.

"Do you recall my warning to you when I last saw you, when you came to the High Krewe's compound in search of blood?" Straussman said to Jules. "I warned you then that you must keep Maureen hidden or risk her resurrection being discovered by the High Krewe. You obviously did not heed my warning in the least. Do you know how *painful* it was for me to learn that Jonathan and Pearl of my household saw Maureen on public access television last evening?"

"Jonathan and Pearl are fans of *The Morganna the Marvelous Show?*" Maureen asked.

"How was I to know those young High Krewe punks even had cable TV?" Jules said.

"The High Krewe's compound may appear to be medieval in structure," Straussman said, "but I assure you, it is well stocked with all of the modern age's conveniences and luxuries. Given Jonathan's voracious nightly consumption of television programs, it was only a matter of time before he stumbled upon Maureen's visage. Honestly, I find myself appalled that the two of you have not seen fit to be more discreet. By placing Maureen on television for the whole world to see, I am afraid you have been unwittingly playing with fire."

"So the High Krewe knows Maureen is back," Jules said, a tone of defiance in his voice. "So *what?* I mean, realistically, what are those lame-ohs gonna do about it?"

"Jules, I wouldn't be so quick to dismiss the High Krewe's capabilities in this matter," the unknown-to-Besthoff fourth person in the room said. "I would listen carefully to whatever Straussman has to share with us."

"Your step-father Dr. Landrieu speaks with wisdom," Straussman said. *Dr. Landrieu — so that is the identity of the medical personage Jonathan warned us that the obese vampire is likely associated with,* Besthoff thought. *Now that I know his name, I can research his background at the computers within our library.* "Now that the Triumvirate know that Maureen has returned, they will want to investigate the methods which were deployed to bring her back out of the netherworld," the butler continued. "And to determine *who* assisted in the deployment of those methods."

"Again I say, *so what?"* Jules said, huffily crossing his fat arms. "The last time the High Krewe wanted somethin' investigated, they had to turn to *me* to do it. Straussman, you honestly think they're gonna ask me to investigate the circumstances of my *own wife's* return from limbo?"

"Don't overly flatter yourself, Jules," Straussman said. "That would be a possibly fatal mistake to make in this instance. The Triumvirate have access to vast funds and a wide network of contacts throughout the vampiric world. Those two factors plainly mean they are not limited to just you in terms of the outside resources they may call upon, first to investigate the facts behind Maureen's return, and then to enact vengeance upon you for stealing the body parts of various young members of their fellowship."

With his own bloodless slips, Straussman confirms what Jonathan and Pearl reported, Besthoff thought to himself in the shadows. *So the fat vampire* was *involved in the pilferage of Victoria's, Flora Ann's, and Alexandra's missing body parts!*

"Excuse me if I ain't exactly tremblin' in my little booties, Straussman," Jules said, his voice laced with disdain. "Who're they gonna get to go after me this time? The black vampires? I don't *think* so. First off, Preston and his crew are still 'vacationing' in St. Louis with that other pack of black vampires who live in the Midwest while their underground den beneath Harrah's Casino gets repaired from the hurricane flooding. Second of all, Preston and me are pretty tight nowadays. I mean, he offered to give me and my family shelter with them in St. Louis right after the storm, when his crew was in the process of pullin' outta town. So there's no *way* he and his pals would agree to go after me and mine, no matter how much money the High Krewe might stack on the table."

"Were you listening to me when I explained about the High Krewe's resources?" Straussman said. "I told you, not only do they have access to a vast amount of money to spend, but they are also tied into a worldwide network of vampires. So if they find they cannot cajole the local black vampires to do their bidding, they can reach out to vampiric confederates from around the globe!"

"All of whom are probably just as lame as they are," Jules said. "I think the events of three years ago pretty much *neutered* your fearsome Triumvirate, pal. They and their youngsters are completely wigged out now at the thought of having anything to do with the big, bad city of N'Awlins. They just wanna take it easy in their luxury compound over by the Jefferson Parish line, put their feet up, and continue slurpin' down that low-fat, low-cholesterol blood they have you and their other flunkies extract from their captive herd of retards."

"Jules, you dangerously underestimate the anger the Triumvirate experienced following the mutilation attacks upon Victoria, Alexandra, and Flora Ann," Straussman said. "I believe they will do all in their not-inconsiderable power to bring vengeance down upon your head and upon the heads of any and all of your friends who also helped with Maureen's resurrection. That means that not only you, but Maureen, Dr. Landrieu, and Rory Richelieu are all in jeopardy."

So the fat vampire's cross-dressing friend was also involved? Besthoff noted. *That is a significant detail — we of the High Krewe maintain considerable financial leverage over Rory Richelieu, since until he has finished making mortgage payments to us, we possess the title on his California institute. It was both foolish and reckless of the New Age guru to risk angering us in this fashion, when we hold the fate of his carefully nurtured business concern in our hands. The list of those who merit our vengeance grows longer by the minute...*

"So what are you suggestin' we do, Straussman?" Jules asked. "Pull up stakes and head out of town? Sell the tour company and retire to some dark corner of Mexico? I mean, bein' perfectly serious now, what would you do if you were in my shoes?"

"I would be exceedingly careful with whom you consort," Straussman suggested. "Be on constant look-out for fellow vampires who sign up for your tours. Those would be the likeliest suspects for the High Krewe's spies and assassins."

"Now hang on just a minute, there, Straussman!" Jules said. "You ain't said nothin' about no *assassins* till now!"

"I would not put it beyond them to hire an assassin to take you and your friends down — particularly if that assassin also has the skills to retrieve the comatose High Krewe members' body parts from Maureen."

"Jules," Maureen said, "now I'm getting *frightened...*"

"All right, Straussman," Jules said, "I guess you can figure you've done your job, now that you've gotten my wife good and scared. Happy now?"

"Please believe me, it was never my intention simply to cause you and Maureen distress. I — I care for her very much, Jules. She is my blood-daughter, the only person in this world to whom I can stake such a claim. Her welfare and happiness will always be paramount for me. I want you to take precautions, no matter how low your opinion of the Triumvirate or the High Krewe may be. I want you *all* to take precautions. Now I must go. I need to pick up some adult diapers and return to my compound before any of the Triumvirate suspect that I have been scheming behind their backs."

Oh, little could you suspect, Straussman, that not only do the Triumvirate suspect your scheming — we now know *your vile culpability and treason. You have gravely disappointed me, blood-son. And now you and your ill-chosen friends must all pay a steep price...*

Four

"I greatly regret to report that we have been nurturing a poisonous, traitorous asp at our breasts." Georges Besthoff stared mournfully down at his carefully trimmed nails as he gave his debriefing to his two fellow members of the Triumvirate within the closed-off quarters of their library. "Johann Straussman, our butler of apparent good standing for the past five centuries, has betrayed us."

"Who *else* ees eenvolved een theese conspiracy to deprive us of our chil-drun?" Nikolas Katz asked.

"Jules Duchon, as you would expect. For his paramour Maureen Remoulade has indeed returned from the netherworld, and, as Jonathan and Pearl surmised, she is the 'beneficiary' of the body parts which have gone missing from our Alexandra, Flora Ann, and Victoria these past three years. The butcher who accomplished the vivisections was a vampire by the name of Dr. Amos Landrieu, former employer of Jules Duchon at the City Morgue, now Duchon's step-father."

"Interesting," Gregory Krauss said.

"Yes, it is. Apparently, from the bits of conversation I was able to pick up while eavesdropping on Straussman and his co-conspirators at the Duchons' residence, Duchon's mother has also returned from the grave in vampiric form and has married this Dr. Landrieu. Even more interesting, from our perspective, is the next member of the conspiracy — Rory 'Doodlebug' Richelieu, Duchon's cross-dressing vampire friend."

"The New Age guru who we financially support?" Krauss said, openly surprised.

"Yes. It was he — or she, if you prefer — who conducted the mystic ceremony which returned Ms. Remoulade from the netherworld so that the vampiric physician could sew together the various body pieces stolen from our company to form a replacement body for her. From what I was able to determine, staring at her from the shadows, the only part of her original form which Ms. Remoulade retains is her own head. Her legs come from Alexandra — I witnessed the mole Jonathan had spoken of. And I also saw other identifying marks, a tattoo of a dragon on Flora Ann's stolen breast and a tattoo of a rose on Alexandra's pilfered arm. If we could recover those stolen body parts from Ms. Remoulade, we could conceivably awaken our three members from their comas by restoring their missing parts to them."

"Doing so, I presume, means doing away with Duchon and this Dr. Landrieu," Krauss said, "and meting out an appropriate punishment to Richelieu?"

"Yes. All that will be necessary in order for us to kidnap Ms. Remoulade and... recover what was stolen from us."

"Vee do not haff the resources on our own to perform such deeds," Katz said, interlocking his bony fingers. "I vill not countenance any reesking of the well-being of our remaining chil-drun. They are *not* to be utilized as keednappers or as keelers."

"Of the remaining servants, I do not judge either Hecht or Otranto to be up to the level of devious craft this assignment calls for," Krauss said. "Particularly not where it concerns their valued coworker of such long standing. Sentiment would get in their way, apart from their lack of skills."

"I concur with both your observations," Besthoff said. "We must look beyond our immediate fellowship. I propose that we adjourn for now and use the remainder of this evening to search our network of contacts for leads to possible outside contractors. Gregory, since you are the most learned among us three at utilizing our computers, I suggest that you take the lead in this."

"I believe I have located an appropriate personage," Gregory Krauss announced the following evening when they next met within their library.

"Tell us about him," Besthoff said.

"Actually, it is a *her*. Before proceeding any further, may I ask your opinion of our working with Orientals? I know we have looked askance at working with vampires of colored African heritage before."

"If she ees anytheeng like Fu-Manchu, she weel be *perfect!"* Nikolas Katz said, clapping his bloodless hands together.

"I won't deign to respond in such a colorful way as my colleague just has," Besthoff said, smiling tightly. "But I have no objections to our hiring someone of Asian ancestry."

"Good. Her name is An Lai Tho. She is a vampiress who currently resides in coastal Texas, but she has family connections within the Vietnamese community of New Orleans East."

"She is an assassin?" Besthoff asked.

"No. She is a *manager* of assassins. When she takes a job, she selects for the work the most suitable killer or killers from among a long list of associates."

"So she sub-contracts out the work?" Besthoff said. "Are all of her subcontractors fellow vampires?"

"Some are. Some are not. Does this present a problem? If it does, I presume we can request that she limit her sub-contracting to vampires only, if that is what you wish."

Besthoff shook his head. "No. I do not wish for us to limit our options. The ideal person for our task may not be a fellow vampire. Let us bring her here to us and see whom she would recommend, given her expertise in such matters."

* * * * *

An Lai Tho arrived at the High Krewe's compound two nights later. Besthoff assisted her with stealthily unloading her coffin from her Ford Econoline van so that she could then park the van in a nearby commercial parking lot; she wanted to avoid calling any attention to herself through having her vehicle occupy space among the High Krewe's motor pool.

Besthoff was immediately impressed by her businesslike tone and her obvious dedication to her assignment. He was also impressed by her petite stature; unlike the High Krewe's women, she was relatively tiny — her forehead barely reached the height of his shoulder. Yet her vampiric strength was obvious from the way she carried her end of the coffin.

"I am sorry that you need to take such precautions," Besthoff said as he helped her set her coffin down within a spare room inside the High Krewe's compound.

"Actually, this is simpler for me than the arduous task of arranging for air shipment and delivery of my coffin while also ensuring discreetness," An Lai said. "It is a more straightforward operation for me to drive my coffin here in my own van. Since I am coming only from Port Arthur, which is less than a five hour drive, and am very familiar with this city, having spent a part of my girlhood here, I prefer to look after my coffin myself."

"I was informed that you have family in New Orleans," Besthoff said. "Vampiric family, or mortal?"

"They are mortal, but are very accepting of me as I am. That is why we are able to maintain regular communication and visitations."

"Very good. I hope your drive here was uneventful?"

"Uneventful and actually rather restful," An Lai said. "I make trips here to New Orleans frequently, so I know the roads very well. A drive through the heart of Manchac Swamp at sixty miles per hour on the I-10 in the dead of night is actually quite refreshing. It gave me time to begin planning my activities here."

"Have you any thoughts on how you intend to proceed?"

"I have formulated some thoughts, yes," she said. "I will be happy to share them with you once I have returned from securing my van. Do you have the telephone number of a taxi company I can call to fetch me back here once I have parked my vehicle?"

Besthoff nodded. "I will have Otranto obtain a number for you."

Besthoff presented their guest to his partners in the library upon her return. "Gregory and Nikolas, allow me to introduce An Lai Tho, the contractor from Port Arthur, Texas whom Gregory has procured to provide us our needed services."

An Lai bowed in a polite, formal mode to Krauss and Katz, as she had already done for Besthoff upon their first meeting. "Thank you for choosing me, oh high and exalted personages of the Triumvirate. I am honored to be of service to you. I wish to hear more of the vampires who will be the victims of the specialist whom I select. This will assist me in making my choice of subcontractors."

"Maureen Remoulade is the primary offender," Krauss said in his high-pitched voice. "For she is the one who dares to 'wear' the body parts which were stolen from our members. Special care must be taken not to damage her in the slightest, for we must have her vivisected so that the stolen body parts she flaunts can be returned safely to the members of our company."

"I see," An Lai said. "That requirement considerably limits the bounds of subcontractors from which I may choose. I will need to hire one who is capable of special finesse. I am glad to know this up front."

"Your most dangerous prey may be Dr. Amos Landrieu," Krauss continued. "He is a physician who we believe originally acted as our youngsters' assailant. He butchered them quite handily, from all accounts. He is not to be trifled with."

"I will make clear note of that," An Lai said.

"On the other hand, your most intellectually astute and wily prey will likely be Rory Richelieu," Krauss continued. "He is the vampire who performed the mystical rite which lured Maureen Remoulade back from the netherworld, so that her head and neck could be attached to our youngsters' body parts. And then there is the vampire who we must assume acted as the ring-leader of this band of miscreants, Jules Duchon— "

"Jules Duchon?" An Lai said, very clearly surprised. "May I have a physical description of this Jules Duchon, please?"

"Surely," Besthoff said, inserting himself into the conversation. "Once seen, Jules Duchon is hardly likely to be forgotten. He is grossly corpulent, weighing at this time somewhere in the region of four to five hundred pounds, I would estimate."

An Lai gasped and covered her mouth with her hand. "He — he is the vampire who turned me," she said.

"Duchon purposefully transformed you into one of us?" Besthoff asked.

An Lai shook her head. "No. I believe it was unintentional, an error on his part. I have been a vampiress for slightly less than three decades now. I — I hired Jules Duchon to drive me home from work in his taxi cab one night, not knowing then what sort of a creature he was. He sealed off the rear compartment of his cab and injected it with a kind of sleeping gas, a laughing gas similar to that which is used in a dentist's office. I was rendered unconscious. While I was unconscious, he drained me of all of my blood. What happened next is a supposition on my part, but I do not know how events could have otherwise played themselves out, seeing that I currently stand before you rather than sitting as a lump of sodden dust on the floor of Manchac Swamp.

"I believe Duchon tried to destroy my brain with a bullet from a gun so that I would not return as a vampiress. I also believe he must have been faulty in his aim, for his bullet failed to sever my brain stem. He dumped my body in Manchac Swamp. The water was so clouded with mud and silt that sunlight did not reach me at all during the three days it took for me to complete my transformation into a vampiress. The mud and silt are what saved me from dissolution. I vaguely remember a thundering pain in my skull as I lay, immobilized, on the floor of the swamp. When I rose at the end of the three nights beneath the light of a mostly full moon, my first instinct upon breaking the water was to take flight. Without consciously directing my next transformation, I changed myself into a bat, and the bullet fell away into the water while my skull was in the misty midst of its transformation into a bat's skull."

"So Duchon has no notion that he has a blood-daughter in you?" Besthoff asked.

"None whatsoever," An Lai said. "Never in these past three decades have I made any attempt to contact him while visiting my family in New Orleans."

"The irony that he will be slain through the efforts of his own blood-daughter is rich, indeed," Krauss said, laughing. "Why, I would have to say it is worth a doubling of your normal fee."

"Actually, given that it is Jules Duchon who is unexpectedly my primary target," An Lai said, "I propose instead to charge you a mere fraction of my normal fee, for this assignment will have special meaning for me. Under other circumstances, I would charge perhaps only half my typical fee. But due to your stipulations, I see I will need to hire a very specialized subcontractor, one who will need to travel all the way from Japan. Given the anticipated additional expense on my part, I am afraid the maximum discount I may prudently offer you is a reduction to three-quarters of my normal fee. I offer this because ending the existence of

Jules Duchon and his confederates will be as much a pleasure as a paid assignment. Is this satisfactory to you?"

"Quite satisfactory, An Lai," Besthoff said, smiling broadly.

Five

SHOGO Fukuda simply *loved* underworld dives like the Sunken Eye. Everything about it harkened back to the Golden Age of Japanese superheroes — the nineteen-sixties and nineteen-seventies, when Japan had been teeming both with costumed superheroes and their opponents, demons and monsters, super-criminals and gangsters. Back then, all sorts of evil creatures and characters had gathered together in underground cabarets such as this one. Now only the gangsters, or *yakuza,* as they preferred to call themselves, remained. But they still preferred, on their off-hours, to congregate in places like the Sunken Eye.

The sultry singer, dressed in a strapless red evening gown, did not have a bad voice, and her choice of songs was top-notch. She also had a pretty nice figure, from what Shogo could see of it through the thick clouds of cigarette smoke which filled the cabaret. But what he loved the most, far more than the singer and the expensive liquor, was eavesdropping on the conversations all around him. That way, he could pretend to be listening in for information about one of the fearsome super-villains who he as Cutie-Scary Man and his partners in the Acme Talent Peerless Proficiencies Trio might have battled back in the day — Hoshimora the Horrible, or the Night Slinker, or the Kamikaze Squad.

Now, of course, these low-level Hiroshima *yakuza* were only involved in petty crimes, mostly victimless crimes such as illegal gambling, smuggling of counterfeit goods from China, and prostitution, crimes which the local or national police could handle. Still, it was great fun for him to imagine that he was listening in on a plot to turn the entire population of Tokyo into mindless zombie slaves to form an invincible army with which to re-invade Korea, or a plan to transform the inhabitants of Kure into sentient slime molds, the type which Hoshimora the Horrible liked to eat.

But then he overheard the whispered word "assassin," followed by a name which truly perked up his ears — "Hiro Matsuba, the Matter Master"...

Matsuba? This was definitely something which Shogo wanted to hear more about. Hiro Matsuba had once been among the greatest of the Japanese superheroes, back in the nineteen-sixties. But once the monsters and evil scientists and super-criminals had been chased out of Japan, many fleeing his very self, he had quickly grown bored with being a mere *tarento,* appearing on television to talk about his past exploits and cutting ribbons at the openings of new government buildings. By the mid-nineteen-eighties, he had turned to a line of work both far more lucrative and much more exciting — being an assassin for hire.

Shogo discreetly changed seats so that he could more easily listen to the gossip which was being shared at the next table. His attention was heightened even more when he heard the words "New Orleans" spoken. Now he was close enough to catch the entire conversation.

"<The Matter Master will make quick work of that bunch in New Orleans, I bet,>" the *yakuza* said in a heavily accented Formosan Japanese.

"<Yes. Can you imagine, though, one group of vampires hiring someone like the Matter Master to rub out another group of vampires? We here in Japan have not heard of such a thing since the 'seventies.>"

An entire group of vampires was in jeopardy from Matter Master's lethal attentions? Could this possibly involve his friends?

The question was resolved for him shortly, when he heard one of the gossipy gangsters say, "<I hear one of the victims is tremendously fat and

will be unable to run from the Matter Master. How I wish I could be there to see such sport!>"

* * * * *

Kenji Tezuka, leader of the Acme Talent Peerless Proficiencies Trio (superhero name: Bonsai Master) felt the color drain from his face as he heard the news which Shogo shared with him. "<Shogo,>" he said in Japanese to his younger cousin at their shared home in Hiroshima, "<this is very dire news which you have just told me. I am glad you have maintained your longstanding contacts with the Japanese underworld. I must try to warn our friend Jules Duchon at once, and I will offer our assistance.>"

His finger trembling with dread, Kenji dialed the phone number which Jules and Maureen had given him three months earlier, before Kenji, his sister Emiko, and their cousin Shogo had departed New Orleans. He checked the clock; it should now be nighttime in New Orleans. He was gratified to hear the corpulent vampire answer the phone on the fourth ring.

"Jures-*san,*" Kenji said in heavily accented English, "this is Kenji Tezuka."

He heard the familiar bass voice on the other end. "*Kenji?* Holy mackerel, what a surprise! Hey, Maureen, you'll never guess who's on the other line! It's our good buddy, Kenji from Japan!"

"Yes, it is very good to hear your voice, too, Jures-*san*. Risten, I have some really *bad* news to share with you. I have heard through my contacts that one of the most powerfuwr of awr the Japanese superpowered *Geinojin* — Hiro Matsuba, otherwise known as *Shina Myoushu,* the feared Matter Master — has been hired by the High Krewe of Vrad Tepes to kiwr you and your friends."

There was a pause on the other end of the line. "Kenji, why should I be afraid of this Matter Master guy? I mean, just three months ago, while I was Mr. Giant White Rabbit, didn't I manage to hold my own while battling with you, Shogo, and Emiko all at the same time? It wasn't easy, but I got through my tussle with you guys without losin' life or limb. What does this guy have on tap that the three of you couldn't toss at me?"

"Matter Master is worthy of fear and respect because he is a throw-back to the owrd days when *Geinojin* were not mere decorative *tarento* who cut ribbons for shopping mawrs. Remember, I towrd you there was a time when *Geinojin* actuary fought monsters and demons and banished creatures such as vampires from the Japanese home isrands. Hiro Matsuba is a veteran of those rong-ago batturs. He remembers awr too wewr what it takes to kiwr a vampire."

"Yeah? Lots of folks know what it takes to kill a vampire — a good dose of sunlight or a wooden stake through the heart. What makes this Matter Master of yours so much more dangerous than any dime-a-dozen, run-of-the-mill vampire hunter?"

"Jures-*san, Shina Myoushu* is a thousand times more deadry than any other known vampire hunter. His is the power to completely con-trowr matter. He could kiwr you or bedevir you in a near-infinite number of ways. Ponder what his sort of power wood awrow him to do to a vam-pire. What does a vampire need to survive? Shewrter from the sun? He cood make a roof turn to transparent grass in the daytime and awrow the sun's rays to boyur away your brud and burn your fresh. He cood turn your coffin into transparent prastic, drag it to an outside rocation, and achieve the same effect. What ewrse does a vampire need? Brud? Oh, the many ways he cood make it impossibur for you to be nourished by brud — he cood transform your fangs into sorrid gawric so that any brud you ingest would be poison to you; or he cood transform the brud you have awrready ingested, the brud inside you, into something which will not feed you, rike red paint. What does a vampire fear? A wooden stake? A hory cross? Hory water? He could transform virtuawry any weapon he has at hand into any of those imprements before you could begin to think of a counter-measure. An even simprer way for him to kiwr you would be to transform you into an inert state of matter, not awrowing you to return to your coffin before daybreak.

"Hiro Matsuba has many years of hard-won experience battring vampires. It is not for just any reason that the Japanese home isrands are entirely devoid of their native brud-suckers. *Shina Myoushu* was a superbry effective exterminator. And now he has been hired to exterminate you and your friends. I offer that the Acme Tarent Peer-ress Proficiencies Trio return to New Orrins to help protect you and your friends from this new threat."

Jules suddenly sounded considerably more interested in the conversation. "So you guys have tussled with Matter Master before? Your super-powers can somehow top his in battle?"

"No, Jures-*san*. I am sad to tewr you, our humburr abirities cannot best those of *Shina Myoushu*. Awrr we can do is beseach him not to harm you."

There was a moment of what Kenji pictured as stunned realization. "You mean *beg* him to leave us alone? Why couldn't you just do that over there in Japan and save yourselves the trip to New Orleans?"

"Hiro Matsuba has many agents and hand-rurs here in Japan. I am shamed to terr you this, but we of the Acme Tarent Peer-ress Proficiencies Trio are not so werr-known in Japan. We wood not be granted audience with *Shina Myoushu*. The ownry hope we wood have of speaking with him wood be to speak with him in New Orrins once he has found you and has shown his face."

"Kenji, pal, not to look a gift horse in the mouth, but I'm perfectly capable of beggin' for my life on my own. Besides, like I've told you, my buddy Doodlebug and me were superheroes ourselves back in World War Two. It's not as if we won't have some tricks up our own sleeves. If the High Krewe has figured out the connection between Maureen and the missing body parts, it's a sure thing they've also got Doodlebug on their hit list, 'cause he's the only one of my buddies who coulda come up with a spell to return Maureen from the netherworld. So Doodlebug has a personal stake in this grudge match, too.

"I really appreciate the offer of an assist, Kenji — and if I thought that assist would take the form of you or Shogo puttin' a fist in this Matter Master guy's chops, I might even take you up on it. But to have you come all the way to New Orleans just to beg for mercy for us? Honestly, Kenji, it ain't dignified — not for you, and not for me, neither. So I'll take your warning that this bad dude is on his way here, and I'll keep both eyes open. But I'll depend on my home-grown buddies to help get us out of this fix, if it's all the same to you, pal."

Kenji swallowed. Hard. He knew he had failed. "I — I understand, Jures-*san*. This is a matter of honor to you. I wirr not interfere any more than I awready have. Good ruck to you, my friend." He hung up the phone.

"<Will Jules and his friends accept our aid?>" Shogo asked.

Kenji slowly shook his head. "<No, my cousin. The fat vampire is a proud being. He will not permit us to go to his home and beg for his life.>"

"<Then he must have the soul of a Japanese,>" Shogo said. "<Death before dishonor. I salute him and his courage.>"

* * * * *

"<Shogo,>" Emiko Tezuka, sister of Kenji Tezuka, whose superhero name was Anime Girl, asked her cousin, "<did my brother have success in convincing our friends in New Orleans to accept our aid?>"

"<No, he did not,>" Shogo answered. "<Jules Duchon is a proud man. When your brother Kenji told him his only recourse was to have Kenji come to New Orleans and beg for his life and the life of his friends, Jules declined his aid.>"

"<You foolish men and your detestable, destructive *pride!*>" Emiko exclaimed. "<Matter Master is far too powerful a foe for Jules to face on his own. He needs all the resources he can muster to come out on top

when faced by such an implacable enemy.>"

"<So how do you intend to ameliorate the situation, my cousin?>" Shogo asked. "<Even your great passion in this matter can accomplish nothing while you remain on this side of the Pacific Ocean.>"

"<That is *exactly* the point I was about to raise to you, Shogo. If Jules will not accept Kenji's above-board aid, then you and I must go to New Orleans to aid him *secretly*. He cannot refuse our help if he does not know we are giving it.>"

"<And how, exactly, do you propose we help Jules Duchon, little cousin?>"

"<I propose we help by locating an ally who will have the brainpower to overcome Matter Master. I must go to New Orleans to find Super-Genius Jules, Shogo — and you and your *otaku* friends must accompany me!>"

Six

SO *Matter Master is coming from Japan to rub me out,* Jules thought, sitting alone on his couch in his living room, pondering what his next moves should be.

It wasn't a comforting notion. Not in the slightest. He felt horribly exposed, as if his making the slightest mistake over the coming weeks would result in the inevitable destruction of all those he held dear (*And y'know, that might just be the case,* he thought). He remembered the bravado he'd passed off as self-assurance on the long distance call he'd shared with Kenji Tezuka three nights ago — his bragging that, since he and Doodlebug had once been superheroes, way back in World War Two, the situation was well in hand.

Had he been absolutely *nuts,* cuckoo, out of his head?

Whatever he was now, he was certainly no superhero. He couldn't avoid admitting that to himself. Sure, there had been superheroes (like Batman, like Captain America) who had been able to be "super" without the benefit of super-powers. But Batman had spent his entire adolescence and young adulthood training himself in a dozen martial arts and learning the techniques and skills of the world's greatest detectives. And Captain America had been dosed with a Super-Soldier serum, which had boosted both his brainpower and his physique to the pinnacle of human perfection, and he worked out constantly, too.

What was Jules without his vampiric abilities? He sure as hell wasn't a Super-Soldier or the World's Greatest Detective, that was certain. Without his vampiric abilities, the very notion that he could even refer to himself as a superhero was just... goofy to the point of absurdity, he realized with a shiver of painful self-knowledge.

For the second time in four years, he needed to man up. He needed to admit to himself that he couldn't survive the next few weeks without Doodlebug, his one-time partner, at his side. And even *with* Doodlebug at his side, it would be a close-run sort of ordeal, one which he might not be able to get through even at his sharpest.

At least it wasn't so hard to make himself call upon Doodlebug for help now. With a sigh of relief, Jules realized he no longer suffered from his former (self-imposed) mental limitation of thinking of Doodlebug's cross-dressing solely as a form of perversity so bizarre as to make his former partner radioactive. What a burden that way of thinking had been — a self-imposed barrier keeping him from one of his oldest and most devoted friends! What idiocy! Had there ever been a way he'd shot himself more grievously in his own foot?

Since the last time he'd needed to call upon Doodlebug for help in such a drastic pinch (when Malice X had threatened to destroy Jules's comfortable lifestyle and kill all his friends in the process), Doodlebug had presided at Jules's and Maureen's wedding. *How much more trust can you set on a guy's shoulders than to have him be the preacher at your wedding?* Jules asked himself. He had fully accepted Doodlebug as his blood-son/daughter. So on this occasion, there would be no delay in seeking Doodlebug's aid. Jules didn't have time to pussyfoot around. He couldn't imagine trusting anybody more than he trusted Doodlebug. Besides that, Doodlebug was in just as much hot water as Jules was. Kenji had said straight out that Jules's former partner in super-heroics was on the High Krewe's rub-out list, too.

So by helping Jules, Doodlebug wouldn't be only saving Jules's blubbery neck. He'd be saving his own skinny, feminine neck, too.

If I want to be anything close *to a superhero again, I gotta pray that*

Doodlebug knows some way to restore my old vampiric powers to me, even after I split bodies with Super-Genius Jules and lost them all. Otherwise, I'm stuck as nothin' better than a 320-pound sittin' duck. And sittin' ducks can't do squat *to save their wife and friends.*

He dialed the long-distance number that would connect him with the compound in Northern California that housed Doodlebug's unique sect, a cult whose members believed they could reach spiritual *nirvana* through regularly cleansing their systems by donating blood to an enlightened vampire. *What a great scam that ol' partner of mine set up for himself,* Jules thought with misty-eyed appreciation. *It's gotta be up there with the all-time classics. It's what inspired me to start my own tour business and fool the tourists into donatin' their blood to me.*

His old friend picked up the phone after it had rung three times. Jules recognized his voice immediately.

"Doodlebug, ol' pal and partner, I gotta ask you one hellavah huge-ass favor. Or maybe it's not so much entirely a favor, you gotta understand, since if things go the way I hope, you'll be gettin' *yourself* outta one hellavah pickle, too..."

"So that's the situation, buddy," Jules finally finished after having kept Rory Richelieu on the phone for the better part of an hour. "We got one bad-ass Japanese assassin sicced on us by those hoity-toity shits at the High Krewe. They wanna steal Maureen's parts back. If I let that happen, I don't have me no wife no more, and your first outing as a marriage preacher might as well as never happened."

"That's a calamity we must prevent at all costs. What do you need me to do? Ask me for anything. *Anything.*"

"If I'm gonna have even a snowball in hell's chance of survivin' this rub-out and rescuin' Maureen, I gotta become a superhero again, Rory. I need to gain back my old vampiric abilities. And you're the only guy on the planet who I think has a whisker of a chance of gettin' 'em back for me. Without my vampiric powers, I'm just a good-for-nothin' 320-pound lump of lard. Stick me in the toaster and set the timer — I'm burnt toast, unless you can figure out how I can start changin' back into my bat-form and my wolf-form and my who-the-hell-knows-what-form."

"That's a tall order, Jules... I'm going to have to do some heavy-duty research into the loss of vampiric powers after a permanent body split... and I can't make you any promises..."

"I don't need no promises. The only assurance I need is that you'll give it your best shot. You gonna at least give it a go?"

"Do I have any other choice? One, you're my blood-father, and I love you, and two, as you put it so nicely, my own neck is on the chopping block as much as yours is, not to mention Maureen's and Amos's. I'll need to spend at least a full night out here consulting my research tomes before I head for New Orleans. I'll phone you back when I know which flight I'll be coming into Louis Armstrong International Airport on, okay?"

* * * * *

Jules didn't even bother greeting Doodlebug properly when he saw him walking down the long arrival corridor at the Louis Armstrong International Airport. "So Rory, did you find anything that'll help me? Do you think you can give me my old powers back?"

Rory "Doodlebug" Richelieu's heart nearly broke when he heard the desperation in his blood-father's voice. Whether Jules accepted it or not, he truly loved the big lug as he would a daddy. He took Jules's elbow and steered him toward the luggage retrieval carousel on the ground floor of the airport, taking care not to stumble in his red pumps, one of his favorite pairs among his almost innumerable shoes. He smoothed the silk of his black dress around his hips while he weaved his old partner around the milling crowds until they found a spot next to the carousel where they could wait for Doodlebug's luggage to slide out of the contrivance's hatch. Flying from California to New Orleans always seemed to leave him a wrinkled mess, but there was nothing to be done about it until he found an iron at Maureen's house. "As I told you over the phone, Jules, I can't make any firm promises. However, I *did* find some promising case studies in my research tomes. Getting back your vampiric abilities after a permanent body split may not be nearly as impossible as I'd originally feared it might be."

His blood-father's face lit up like a nighttime sky during New Year's Eve at midnight. "Really? You ain't shittin' me none? You think you can really *do* it?"

"The key to it, just like when I tried to convince you three years ago that you could separate yourself into more than one form at a time, is your own belief system, Jules. Specifically in this case, your belief that splitting off a second body would mean you would forever lose your vampiric powers."

"Ya mean to tell me that ain't *true?"*

"Oh, it's *partially* true, Jules. But the primary side-effect of splitting off a second body, a vampire's loss of his ability to morph into other forms, is a *temporary* phenomenon. Your body — well, it adjusts over time."

"If that's the case, then what's my problem?" Jules asked.

"Your problem is that you believe so strongly that you shouldn't have your powers — so you *don't* have them. Do you remember from three years ago when I told you that the primary, in fact one of the only, limitations on a vampire's ability to shift forms is his own belief system? Do you remember asking me why vampires of European descent could transform into bats, wolves, and rats, but vampires of African descent could transform themselves into panthers and hyenas, but not bats or wolves?"

"Uh, yeah, I guess I do," Jules mumbled.

"Well, if you recall, I explained to you that vampires of African descent were able to transform themselves into panthers and hyenas because hundreds of years' worth of folklore had *told them* they could transform themselves into panthers and hyenas. Just as hundreds of years of folklore had told European vampires that they could transform into bats, wolves, and rats. When it comes to vampires and their powers, Jules, the vampire's belief system shapes the range of his abilities, not the other way around."

"So you're sayin' if I just believe I've got my powers back, I will? That sounds too easy, Rory."

"Oh, it's not easy at all," Doodlebug said sadly. "The hard part is actually *getting* you to believe it."

"But I gotta figure you wouldn't have flown all the way out here without a plan as to how to do that," Jules said in a voice filled with hopefulness.

"Indeed I do," Rory said. "We must mentally return you to a time when you had absolutely no doubts about your vampiric powers. We must utilize *hypnosis,* my dear friend. Hypnosis and a good dose of role-playing — that's my prescription for what ails you."

"I have to dress up as *what?"* Maureen screeched. "And wear this black wig, too?"

"It'll only be for a few nights," Doodlebug said. Again, he tried handing her the box which contained her costume. "Only as long as it takes to convince Jules that he is back in World War Two, fighting alongside his old allies. Then his powers should kick back in, and we can all drop the masquerade."

"So you're telling me I've gotta dress up as *Wondrous Woman?* And I've gotta *stay* dressed as Wondrous Woman for at least a couple of nights? But Doodlebug, I've got to do my show. I can't dress as Wondrous Woman. I've got to dress as Morganna the Marvelous..."

"Hon," Jules said from the sofa of his living room, "if I don't get my powers back, and in a hurry, and if we don't start gettin' *real* lucky *real* soon, you might have no reason to dress up as Morganna the Marvelous ever again. 'Cause you'll be *dead again* and stuck in the netherworld.

You get me?"

Amos "Doc" Landrieu also glanced dubiously at the costume which Doodlebug had handed him. "And I'm also supposed to play dress-up? You have me dressing up as — who is it again?"

"Doctor Supernatural."

"He was an actual superhero from World War Two? I've never heard him."

"Not too many people have," Doodlebug said. "He mostly worked deeply undercover. But he emerged on one occasion to help Jules and me with one of our cases while we were in our costumed identities as the Hooded Terror and Doodlebug."

Doc Landrieu removed the costume from its box and draped it over himself to check its sizing. "So you're saying my dressing up as this 'Doctor Supernatural' is absolutely necessary for this hypnosis to work?"

"I can't say it's absolutely necessary, Amos," Doodlebug said. "But the more of his old allies we can surround Jules with while I attempt to trigger the resumption of his former powers, the better."

* * * * *

Doodlebug finished placing Jules into deep hypnosis. When Jules opened his eyes once more, he had gone back in time over seventy years, and he saw reality through the frayed eye-holes of the Hooded Terror's leather hood.

Where was he? Why was he in a gymnasium?

The Hooded Terror glanced around him. Why was he here? His pulse raced a little less quickly once he identified three of his closest allies — Wondrous Woman, Doctor Supernatural, and of course his own loyal partner, Doodlebug the Marvel Boy. Doctor Supernatural was dressed in his typical green double-breasted suit, trench coat, and slouch hat. Wondrous Woman was dressed in her regulation red, white, and blue form-fitting leotard, which showed off her ample curves to, *ahem,* great effect. But Doodlebug...?

Something was *off* about Doodlebug's costume. The Hooded Terror struggled to pin down the difference he somehow just *knew* was there. The colors were right: yellow body suit, purple domino mask, purple leggings, and black boots. But when had Doodlebug started wearing white calf-skin gloves?

And then there were his own cloak and hood. Why did they feel so... *confining,* all of a sudden?

"He's fighting the hypnosis," the Hooded Terror overheard his partner whispering to Wondrous Woman. "What could be the matter?"

"I think it's your costume," Wondrous Woman whispered back to Doodlebug. "It's not exactly the same one you wore during the war, is it?"

The Hooded Terror was mystified. What could this cryptic exchange between two of his closest allies possibly *mean?*

"I see you're feeling, ah, a bit *confused,* maybe, Hooded Terror?" Doodlebug said to him in a normal voice. "That's an after-effect of the drug that our Japanese enemy Tora, Tora, Tora dosed you with. The drug that, ah, stole away your vampiric powers. That's why we brought you to this gym, Hooded Terror. I'm going to train you so that you can fight off the effects of that vile Axis-created drug and *remember* how to use your powers."

"*You're* gonna train *me* in the use of my vampiric powers?" the Hooded Terror said. "Don't you have that backwards, Doodlebug, my minuscule teenaged partner in fighting crime and Nazi sabotage? Aren't *I* the one who showed *you* how to transform into a bat, et cetera, et cetera?"

"Just go with it, Hooded Terror," Wondrous Woman said, a hint of exasperation in her normally sweet and upbeat all-American voice.

"Well, okay," the Hooded Terror said. "I guess I *am* a little confused, so I'll just roll with whatever you guys suggest I do."

"That's a good Hooded Terror," Wondrous Woman said. Mysteriously, it sounded to the Hooded Terror as though she were addressing him as a dog.

"Okay, Hooded Terror, I want you to climb up that rope to the gym's ceiling," Doodlebug said.

The Hooded Terror stared dubiously at this latest obstacle which his partner Doodlebug had arranged (seemingly to no purpose but to bedevil him). "You want me to do *what?* I can't shimmy up that rope like I was some kinda lizard or somethin'! What do you take me for?"

"You're a superhero with all the powers of a vampire," Doodlebug insisted firmly, as though he were trying to pound this notion into the Hooded Terror's brain with a wooden mallet. "Climbing that rope would pose *no problem* to you if you would just *allow* yourself to transform into a bat or a rat— "

"Wait a minute, that don't make no sense," the Hooded Terror said hastily. "What's this about I hafta 'allow' myself to transform into a bat or a rat?"

"The, uh, the drug that Tora, Tora, Tora slipped you negates your powers by making you falsely believe that you don't have them anymore," Doodlebug said. "So when I say you must 'allow' yourself to transform, what I mean is you must *believe* that you can still transform. Only your belief can counteract the drug."

The Hooded Terror curled his lip. "That sounds like a whole buncha hoity-toity psychological mumbo-jumbo to me, lil' partner."

"Hooded Terror, sometimes even mumbo-jumbo can work like magic. Just trust me, please!"

"Aww, hell, I been trustin' my life to you ever since I first turned you into my wee little vampiric sidekick, Doodlebug," the Hooded Terror said. "I guess it won't hurt me none to keep on trustin' you for a while yet, will it?"

The Hooded Terror noticed that Doctor Supernatural appeared very nervous now that they were out scouting the grounds of the Higgins Boat Factory alongside Bayou St. John. He wished he could reassure his comrade-in-arms that Tora, Tora, Tora wouldn't have a prayer against the super-heroic might of all three of them.

"Rory — uh, Doodlebug — are you sure it's a *good idea* for us to be out in the open like this?" Doctor Supernatural said. "Aren't we making ourselves prime targets?"

"We need to, uh, shock Hooded Terror into remembering that he still retains his powers," Doodlebug said.

Geeze, the Hooded Terror thought to himself, *they're all constantly walkin' on egg shells when they're around me. I just wish everybody would lighten up...*

"Hey, who pulled the big practical joke?" the Hooded Terror said when he realized the Higgins Boat Factory wasn't where it was supposed to be, on the banks of Bayou St. John across from City Park. "Which one of you has the super-power to make a whole factory disappear?"

"Uh, the threat of Tora, Tora, Tora must've convinced the authorities to move the Higgins Boat Factory to a different, secret location," Doodlebug reassured him. "That's why, uh, we didn't think it was the greatest idea for us to come out here. That's why Doctor Supernatural and Wondrous Woman are so nervous."

He ain't tellin' me the truth, the Hooded Terror thought glumly. *But why do I have a sneakin' suspicion that the truth will set me free?*

"Now how are we super-heroes supposed to guard a munitions factory when the authorities don't even see fit to tell us where it is?" the

Hooded Terror asked (it was actually a rhetorical question; he didn't expect an answer).

"I'm sure 'Tora, Tora, Tora' could answer that one," Wondrous Woman said to Doodlebug with a smirk that confounded the Hooded Terror. "Doodlebug, your plan is working out just *peachy* so far. Is it really *vital* that Hooded Terror gets his super-powers back?"

"It might mean the difference between his living and his dying," Doodlebug said mournfully.

The Hooded Terror nearly yanked off his hood with frustration. *Why the hell is everybody so down in the dumps all the time?* he thought. *They act like they're headin' for somebody's funeral...*

Seven

"HIRO Matsuba, honorable *Shina Myoushu,* most skilled and powerful of the *Geinojin,* allow me the pleasure of officially welcoming you to New Orleans, the venerable site of your next assignment," An Lai Tho said when she greeted the Japanese assassin at Louis Armstrong International Airport.

Matsuba returned the Vietnamese vampiress's formal bow. He was a powerfully built man, whose musculature belied his advanced age; the only sign of his true age which An Lai could see was the glorious garland of silver hair which crowned his head, silver hair which contrasted so winningly with his dark eyes. "It is my honor," he said in English only slightly inflected with a Japanese accent, "to be able to make myself of service to an employer who has always treated me favorably and fairly, and who compensates me generously for my labors."

"Compensation for us both will not be lacking in this instance," An Lai said, thinking of the pleasure she would derive from having her abominable blood-father killed. As on previous occasions when she had met Hiro Matsuba, his aura of masculine force nearly overwhelmed her; like so often before, she asked herself, *Do I select him for assignments because of his unique abilities, or do I select him because I so enjoy being in his awesome presence?* "The High Krewe of Vlad Tepes are among the wealthiest vampires on Earth. This case that I now set you upon is more than a mere cause for them — it is a blood-feud. They intend to go to war with the man who served as my blood-father."

"Does this notion cause you any trepidation?" the assassin asked, watching her expression intently. "I should prefer to know if it does."

An Lai laughed, a motion which she knew displayed the pearl-white flesh of her throat most appealingly. "No, *Shina Myoushu,* there is no love to be lost between my blood-father Jules Duchon and me. Now come. Unless you wish to stop for a *café au lait,* the coffee and steamed milk which is one of the delicacies of New Orleans, we will collect your luggage, and I will take you directly to the compound of the High Krewe of Vlad Tepes."

The assassin shook his head. "I have no need of caffeine," he said. "I am fully awake and ready to serve."

An Lai ushered her colleague into the High Krewe's library. "Distinguished members of the Triumvirate, allow me to introduce to you Hiro Matsuba, known as *Shina Myoushu,* or in English, the Matter Master. Matsuba-*san* is renowned the world over as the most skilled and powerful of the *Geinojin,* that corps of Japanese superheroes who earned their fame during the nineteen-sixties and nineteen-seventies banishing all criminal and monstrous elements from the Japanese home islands. During his heyday, he was the star of numerous anime films which celebrated his prowess and dramatized his battles against demons, criminals, and vampires. After the successful expulsion of all such antisocial and supernatural threats from Japan, he then spent a decade and a half performing as a *tarento* in Japan, hiring himself out to cut ribbons at the openings of new governmental buildings and such. If I may be so unhumble as to call attention to one of my greatest achievements, I successfully convinced *Shina Myoushu* to emerge from this slightly undignified retirement and pursue a new career as an assassin-for-hire, focusing primarily on the types of super-criminal and supernatural opponents he battled against in the 'sixties and 'seventies — with the great differences being that, unlike before, he pursues these opponents around the world, not merely within the confines of Japan; and when he battles them, he ensures that the battle ends in the finality of his opponent's death or permanent disablement, not mere banishment. He has found this new, third career to be both satisfying and lucrative, far more so than his second career as a *tarento*."

Georges Besthoff bowed to his new guest, then shook his hand. He handed Hiro Matsuba a set of dossiers, packets of background information on each of his intended victims. "Welcome to New Orleans, Matter Master," he said. "I have taken the time to prepare background dossiers on each of your targets — Jules Duchon, Maureen Remoulade, Rory Richelieu, Amos Landrieu, and one of our own employees, Johann Straussman. Please take a few minutes to review them, and then let us know if any of the contents of these background folders raise any questions or concerns."

Matter Master took but a few moments to read through the contents of the various folders. He looked up at Besthoff and grunted with satisfaction. "Thank you for preparing these, Besthoff-*san*," he said. "It is good for me to be familiar with my targets prior to my beginning my assignment."

"Did anything you read raise any concerns?"

Hiro Matsuba smiled and shook his head. "No. These are all rather common-type targets to be assigned to me for elimination. The only opponent who might manage to present me with any challenge at all could be Rory Richelieu, since, according to the materials you have presented to me, in addition to his being a vampire, he dabbles in the dark arts of necromancy and sorcery. However, during my long career, I have battled both demons and self-styled wizards, so I will face Rory Richelieu without any great forebodings in my breast."

"That is a declaration of great confidence," Gregory Krauss said. "Before we set you loose in the field, I would greatly appreciate a demonstration of your power."

"That is easily enough done," Matter Master said. He seized one of the library's end tables in his powerful hands and concentrated intently upon its form. Luminescent green energy arced from his hands into the wood of the table. Before the astounded eyes of the Triumvirate, the table was transformed into a large standing statue of a bat. "Bring me the first of my targets," he said, "the one who is your employee, and I shall replace your missing table for you."

Besthoff nodded. "I shall summon Johann Straussman."

He pressed a red button which was set into the wall. A few minutes later, the butler quietly entered the library. He stared suspiciously from the faces of his three masters to the faces of the two unknown guests. "Yes?" he said hesitantly. "How may I be of service this evening?"

"You may be of service by becoming part of this library's stock of furniture, servant," Matter Master said. Before Straussman could flee, he grabbed the butler's arm. Just as it had only a moment before, green energy arced from his hands to Straussman's pale, bloodless flesh. Before the startled vampire could utter a cry, he was transformed into an end table.

An Lai felt her knees go slightly weak. She always had this reaction when watching *Shina Myoushu* exercise his almost godly abilities. It was like standing in the presence of a deity. Who could possibly overcome her chosen agent? He was invincible.

"It appears our Vietnamese interlocutor has selected her assassin well," Gregory Krauss said with obvious satisfaction. "I must congratulate myself on the foresight I displayed when I made my choice." The High Krewe's library echoed with the sounds of Krauss vigorously patting himself on the back.

An Lai had re-dressed in a loose-fitting robe, a garment which could easily be discarded. Beneath the robe, nothing else covered her vampiric flesh. She shivered slightly in the cool fall air. Vampires, whose temperature always reflected that of their surroundings, reveled in summer and dreaded winter, although many chose to endure it for the sake of a well-stocked hunting territory.

Now she stood, almost naked, in the luxurious courtyard of the High Krewe's compound, a broad space of well-tended grass and flowers, whose centerpiece was a massive fountain containing a tall column topped with a platform holding a statue of a bat (not so different from the statue the Matter Master had created from the library table). Facing her, dressed in the loose-fitting combat kimono which he preferred for such exercises, stood Hiro Matsuba.

"Matsuba-*san,*" An Lai said, "will you mind the sight of my naked flesh? It will be necessary to discard this robe in order to exercise my vampiric powers and provide you with a training exercise."

The Matter Master smiled and crossed his arms confidently. "Why would I mind such a pleasant sight? But I must ask you, Tho-*san,* is this truly necessary? After all, I have battled vampires many times before."

"But by your own admission, it has been a number of years since you faced a vampire. And on this assignment, you may be required to battle several vampires at once. I always want my employees to be as well-prepared as is humanly possible — or in your case, as is super-humanly possible. Do you agree?"

"I will bow to your wisdom in this, Tho-*san.*"

"Good."

An Lai untied the belt of her robe and allowed it to drop to the ground. She noticed the Matter Master's obvious appreciation of her naked figure, with its small but well-formed breasts and slender hips. *He will have only seconds in which to admire me,* she thought. *For I intend to give him no quarter — I will fight as though this were a fight to the death, and I shall see how ready, or how rusty, he is.*

She quickly transformed herself into a giant bat, one with a five-foot wingspan. She flew straight at his eyes, intending to gouge them out with her powerful claws. He parried her attack with several well-aimed karate chops, keeping her claws from his face. But her claws did manage to rake his right forearm, leaving bloody traces behind. First blood to her.

Then she flew down to the base of the fountain and scooped up two bricks which the servants had been preparing to cement into the base as part of a repair. Straining her wings to the utmost, she soared above the top of the tall fountain and prepared to dive bomb the Matter Master and drop the bricks on his head, aiming to stun him or perhaps even give him a concussion.

She caught him following her with his eyes. Then she was momentarily blinded by a dazzling flash of green energy. When her weak eyes cleared from their bedazzlement, she saw that his skin had changed color. It was now a silver-gray.

She dove down at him and dropped the two bricks. Her aim was true — they both struck him in the head. Yet each brick shattered into dust.

Hiro Matsuba laughed. "A fine shot you have taken, Tho-*san!*" he called up to her. "But what good are mere bricks, even dropped from a great height, against skin made of titanium?"

Yes, he is also the master of his own *matter, the matter of his own body,* she told herself. *I forgot this. But he could not have transformed his eyes into titanium, or he would be blind. His eyes remain his weakness.*

After hovering the half-second it took her to decide upon her next course of action, she resumed her dive, this time aiming her claws once more straight at his eyes. He did not bother resorting to karate to respond to this attack. He simply covered his eyes with one invincible hand, completely shielding them from her claws.

If only he will retain that position covering his eyes for another few seconds, I may be able to surprise him.

She silently landed a few feet behind him, then concentrated on pulling more of her temporarily discarded mass through the null dimension. She transformed immediately into a great white wolf, with no transitional change into human form. Then, while he was still blindly protecting himself from her bat claws, she leaped upon his back and toppled him to the ground.

She used her powerful neck muscles and forepaws to roll him over. Then she dove for his eyes, her fangs, coated with saliva, flashing in the moonlight, her lupine orbs filled with animal fury. But he moved more quickly than she would have thought possible, particularly for a man who had transformed his skin into titanium armor. He grabbed her by the scruff of her neck and hurled her across the courtyard.

She managed to roll with the impact of landing and quickly regained her footing. *He has done well thus far,* she thought. *But I am determined to show him* all *that a vampire is capable of.*

She noted the direction of the breeze. It was blowing from behind her towards Matter Master. She concentrated the fullness of her mental abilities and reduced her density to its lowest possible point, becoming a noxious mist. The breeze blew her towards her opponent/employee. She surrounded him, concentrating the bulk of her gaseous form around his head. She wormed her way into his nostrils and through his lips, down into his lungs, crowding out the air.

After thirty seconds of not being able to breathe, he fell to the ground. Another green flash illuminated the courtyard. Hiro Matsuba's metal armor returned to its normal state as human flesh.

An Lai transformed back into her human shape. She bent down over his now-vulnerable neck, intending to bite him while he was unconscious and drink a pint or two of his blood — not wishing to kill him or change him into a vampire, merely wanting to temporarily disable him and thus prove to him that more such practice sessions were required before he entered the hunting fields against a whole group of vampires.

But he opened his eyes and suddenly smiled. *Has he been playing possum?* she managed to think before he reached up and touched her with his right hand. After that, she could remember nothing, not until he restored her to her normal form a moment later.

"What... what happened?" she asked, feeling weak and drained. "What did you do to me?"

"I transformed you into a most delectable ice sculpture," Matter Master said. "Had I wished it, I could have left you thus and allowed you to melt, then sink into the grass as water, never to be seen again. But I value you too much as an employer. Do you agree that I am fully ready to battle vampires, Tho-*san*?"

An Lai found it impossible to disagree.

Eight

EMIKO decided to waste no time once she and her cousin Shogo arrived in New Orleans. As soon as they had taken a taxi from the Louis Armstrong International Airport to the downtown Residence Inn and checked into their room, she began changing out of her travel clothes and into her superheroine costume.

"<Emiko,> Shogo said, staring at her with dubious eyes, "<why must you do this now? We have just completed an exhausting flight from Japan which has taken us slightly more than a full day. Why don't you sleep for a time, and *then* search for Hiro Matsuba, the Matter Master?>"

Emiko shook her head fervently. "<No, Shogo! Every hour we tarry increases the possibility that we will be unable to help Jules, his family, and his friends! It has already been days since Kenji learned that the Matter Master has been hired to assassinate them all. I must do two things. I must discover whether the Matter Master has already arrived in New Orleans, and I must strive to locate Super-Genius Jules, who will be able to help his twin, if only we can convince him to do so. Shogo, you must permit me to drain energy from one of your stored, miniaturized fan-boys. Right now. In this instance, Kenji and I will forgive your selfish practice of carrying them around with you as batteries to spark up your super-powers, rather than immediately returning them to their normal forms after one of our performances in Hiroshima.>"

Shogo frowned and slowly nodded. He was not especially happy with

Emiko using her super-powers so soon after such an exhausting transcontinental flight, but he decided it would be fruitless to argue with her any further. He knew his cousin's stubborn streak all too well. "<Very well, my diminutive cousin,>" he said. "<While you finish changing into your super-heroine costume, I will retrieve one of the miniaturized fan-boys from my luggage so that you may use him as a battery to spark your super-powers.>"

Shogo went to the hotel room's closet and retrieved a special, custom-made padded case. This padded case was perforated with dozens of air holes and, from the outside, looked like an ordinary pet caddy (he had taken it aboard the aircraft as a piece of carry-on luggage and had placed it beneath the seat in front of him). He opened the padded case; it was filled with six oblong wooden boxes, each about six inches long. Each of the boxes was also perforated with air holes. Glowing green energy shined through the air holes of four of the boxes. Shogo smiled to himself; he had never realized it before, but the oblong boxes looked like miniature coffins, as though the *otaku* resting inside were tiny glowing vampires. How ironic that he should utilize a person who looked so much like a miniaturized vampire sleeping in his coffin to possibly help rescue a group of real vampires!

He removed one of the oblong boxes and opened it, then gently removed the sleeping *otaku* and carefully laid him down upon one of the hotel room's twin full-size beds. He knew the *otaku,* glowing a brilliant green color, wasn't truly asleep; he was in a sort of a coma, from which he would emerge only when Shogo restored him to his full size and close to his original mass (part of his mass would have been expended as energy, sparking up Emiko's super-powers).

Shogo reviewed the serial metamorphoses of the *otaku* in his head. All of the *otaku* were volunteers, fan-boys and fan-girls so incredibly enamored of the Acme Talent Peerless Proficiencies Trio that they were willing to serve for a short while as living batteries. First, Kenji miniaturized them and gained super-energy from converting their missing mass into energy which he absorbed into his body. Then he passed along nearly all of that super-energy to his sister Emiko, who kissed the tiny *otaku* and turned him *kawaii*-cute, into the image of whatever adorable anime character she wished, at the same time restoring nearly all of the super-energy to the *otaku*. Then the *otaku* was passed along to Shogo, who absorbed the super-energy residing within the otaku and used that super-energy to spark his own super-transformations.

The energy could be passed between the members of the *tarento* trio in other permutations, too. But the last step in the chain of energy transfers was invariably when Shogo returned the bulk of the super-energy to the *otaku* by changing him back into his original form. The only thing the *otaku* lost was twenty to thirty pounds, depending on how much super-energy the Acme Talent Peerless Proficiencies Trio had consumed in performing their various transformations and uses of their super-powers. Shogo's cousin Kenji never allowed very skinny *otaku* to volunteer, because they could not afford the loss of twenty or thirty pounds without becoming dangerously frail.

But the three *otakus* in Shogo's special padded case and the one now lying on the bed had secretly volunteered for even more super-heroic involvement than *otaku* usually did. Shogo had surreptitiously met with them prior to one of the Acme Talent Peerless Proficiencies Trio's performances in Hiroshima and asked whether they wished to assist him on "secret missions." These four had been thrilled at the thought; Shogo knew they all looked forward to sharing their adventures in their amateur *otaku* manga comics and YouTube journals and swapping stories at their conventions. At the time, he had lied to them about the secret missions part, wanting them only to spark up his private uses of his super-powers. But now, ironically enough, he and his cousin Emiko were engaged in an *actual* secret mission, and Shogo realized he had unwitting told these four *otakus* the truth.

Shogo noticed that Emiko had not put on her entire superheroine uniform. "<Emiko, what about your ruffled skirt?>"

"<I only wear the skirt for public performances,>" she said. "<When I have to go into action, like now, the minimal uniform is best.>" She had dressed in the Acme Talent Peerless Proficiencies Trio's standard silver body suit with matching silver calf-length boots. Now she put on something she didn't normally wear — a domino mask. "<In case you are wondering, I put on the domino mask so that if anyone sees me appear on their screen, they will think I am an actress in a superhero show. Shogo, please retrieve my laptop computer and log onto this hotel's wi-fi. Then I can begin my searches, with the help of your *otaku* friend on the bed.>"

"<Very well. I will do so, cousin. But are you absolutely certain you want to strain yourself so mightily this soon after our transcontinental flight?>"

Emiko nodded. Shogo sighed to himself, but he dutifully went to retrieve the laptop case from the closet. He placed the laptop on the room's desk, plugged it in, and logged onto the hotel's wi-fi service.

"<We're connected,>" he said.

Emiko nodded again. She picked up the miniaturized *kawaii otaku* from the bed and placed her lips against his tiny cheek. Rivulets of green-tinged energy arced from the *otaku*'s glowing form through Emiko's lips and then throughout the rest of her body.

The *otaku* stopped glowing. But now Emiko appeared to be lit by a green light which flickered from inside her lithe form. "<I'm ready, Shogo.>" Shogo stood aside, and Emiko approached the desk. She stood before the computer and concentrated mightily. With a flash of green energy, she became a two-dimensional cartoon version of herself. She slithered across the floor, up the desk's leg, and onto the desk's surface. Then she slid from the desk into the computer screen and instantly disappeared into the ether.

Shogo knew that, when she was traveling in her Anime Girl form through wireless connections that could include computers, Internet-capable televisions, smart phones, and even the GPS units mounted in car dashboards, she was traveling at the speed of electromagnetic energy — the speed of light. Peering out from the insides of hundreds of thousands of device screens, she could conduct searches in seconds of New Orleans that would take her weeks, if not months, should she try to accomplish them on foot.

Four seconds later, she rematerialized within the computer screen, not even breathing hard. "<I went to the security network of the High Krewe of Vlad Tepes, which is connected into a localized computer network, which is in turn connected to a wide-area computer network. I saw the Matter Master. He is here in New Orleans.>"

"<Emiko, did you learn anything about his plans—?>"

He let his question trail off. Before he had said more than two words, she had vanished into the ether again.

This time, he waited an hour and twenty minutes for her to reappear. In the meantime, he turned on the History Channel and became engrossed in a documentary about a Japanese soldier who had grown old on a Pacific Island, still believing the war between Japan and the United States was ongoing.

She reappeared on the computer screen when he wasn't looking and called out to him, "<I'm back!>" He was greatly startled. He hated that reaction, which made him feel like a child. But there was no arguing the point that a woman reappearing in one's hotel room when one is engrossed in a documentary about a Japanese soldier still fighting World War Two could be very disconcerting. Then, in a flash of green energy, she reassumed her three-dimensional form, now sitting on the desk.

She appeared spent. She fell upon the bed closest to the sliding glass door and balcony and rolled over on her back so she could speak with him. "<I am sorry I took so long,>" she said. "<I am *so* tired. I was searching for Super-Genius Jules. I must have circled the city's Internet connected screens a hundred times, looking aimlessly and randomly for the twin of Jules Duchon. I only found him by happenstance. A tourist was

performing an Internet search on her smart phone when I spotted Super-Genius Jules.>"

"<Where is he? Did you speak with him?>"

"<No, I dared not rematerialize from the smart phone. I would have given the owner a heart attack. But Super-Genius Jules isn't far from this place. He is earning money acting as a fortune teller on Jackson Square.>"

They took a cab to Jackson Square. The bright half-moon seemed to follow them as they drove through the old streets of the Vieux Carré. They found Super-Genius Jules sitting by the iron fence which surrounded the square. He was seated behind a folding table which held a deck of tarot cards and a price list. Shogo mentally added a hundred and forty additional pounds to that face and body, and Super-Genius Jules was the mental spitting image of standard-issue Jules Duchon — with the exception of his bizarrely elongated head, which housed his gargantuan brain. But right now, that elongated head was hidden beneath a stovepipe hat, one which made him look either like a circus ringmaster or the fortune teller he was pretending to be.

Shogo saw a smile briefly appear on Super-Genius Jules's face. "Ah, Shogo and Emiko," Super-Genius Jules said, palming his tarot cards. "To what do I owe this rare pleasure? Please don't tell me you've come to capture me and somehow force me to re-merge with my mentally challenged twin. We've been through that already. Would you like your fortunes told, in any case?"

"We want neither," Emiko said. "Your merging with standard Jures now would end up with a singurar Jures who would be easy to kiwr. We need your super-interrigence. We need you to herrp Jures and his famiry. They are under the threat of assassination from Hiro Matsuba, *Shina Myoushu—* "

"The Matter Master. Yes, I'm familiar with him. For one thing, I speak passable Japanese; I learned it in a few minutes from a Berlitz course I checked out from the library. For another, I just watched that terribly uncreative anime movie called *Matsuba, Matter Master*. I watch Maureen's show whenever I can; I do miss her. When it comes to films, she picks the lowest of the low to lampoon. What poor production values in that anime 'extravaganza!' Oh, in case you're wondering, I'm also aware that the real Hiro Matsuba has been working as a super-powered assassin-for-hire for the past twenty-two years. I did some quick research on him, finding him interesting after watching that wretched movie. Prior to his work as an assassin, he toiled for small-time pay as a *tarento,* I believe, cutting ribbons at newly opened shopping malls and the lot. So what is it you would like to ask me to do, Emiko and Shogo?"

"We need you to use your super-interrigence," Shogo said, "to figure out a way to defeat the Matter Master before he can kiwr our friends."

Super-Genius Jules briefly pursed his lips. "Now why on Earth would I have any motivation at all to save my mentally feeble twin? I have been working here in Jackson Square so that I can spy upon his nightly activities when he leads his tours. He is nothing more than an inferior facsimile of me, despite being my creator. The creation has surpassed his creator — *I* am the superior Jules Duchon. I am the one who deserves to continue to live, not that bumbling, obese fool of a vampire. Should he vanish from the face of the Earth — 'no skin off my nose,' as that pithy little saying goes."

"But you have just said a reason why you shood try to defeat the Matter Master," Shogo said. "Even if you are the superior Jures Duchon, you are still a part of Jures Duchon. You are made from his body. If the Matter Master discovers your existence, he wirr be ordered by the High Krewe of Vrad Tepes to kiwr you, too."

"The High Krewe? So *they* are the pathetic bunch who arranged the hit on my obese twin? I didn't think they had the testicular fortitude. Now *why* would they possibly have reason to kill Jules Duchon...?" Shogo saw his face light up with sudden understanding. "Ah-*ha!* They must have discovered Maureen's reappearance, perhaps by seeing her host *The Morganna the Marvelous Show* on public access television. And they must have seen some tell-tale clue which indicated she was resurrected with the aid of various body parts stolen from young women of the High Krewe. Of course, they would assume Jules Duchon was complicit in this crime. Am I correct?"

"We do not know the detaiwrs of why Maureen has been targeted for death," Emiko said. "Kenji did not know and so cood not tewr us. But we *do* know for certain that Maureen is on the assassination rist. So if you ruvv her, Super-Genius Jures, you must try to save her by using your great brain to figure out a way to defeat the Matter Master."

Super-Genius Jules rubbed his chin. "Hrrmm... you have given me much to think about. He *does* have a weakness which can be exploited. I will need to ponder this. Where are you staying so that I can reach you once I have made my decision?"

"At the downtown Residence Inn," Shogo said.

Their next stop was the home of Maureen and Jules Duchon. They hadn't bothered to take a cab; the townhouse they were seeking was only a few blocks' walk through the night-dark streets from Jackson Square.

Shogo rang the bell. Jules answered. But it quickly became apparent to Shogo that their sizable friend was not at all in his right mind.

"Who—?" Jules mumbled. Then he stared at Emiko and Shogo with a cockeyed look of partial recognition. "Wait a minute... I *know* you two from somewheres! You, the girl — your name is Emiko. And that guy there — that's Shogo — he's your cousin, right?"

"Yes, of course, Jures-*san*," Emiko said, looking to her cousin with confusion. "Of *course* you know us! We have come awr the way from Japan to warn you! Jures-*san*, you must run from this city with your friends! The most terriburr assassin of them awr, Matsuba, *Shina Myoushu* — Hiro Matsuba, the feared Matter Master — has arrived in New

Orrins from Japan to kiwr you and your famiry! But there is someone who can herrp you — your super-smart twin, Super-Genius Jures, has returned from the bottom of the ocean and is working as a fortune teller in the prace you cawr Jackson Square— "

"Wait, wait," Jules said, peering suspiciously from Shogo to Emiko and back again, "I think I get it now! I know you two 'cause you been livin' in New Orleans as a maid and a gardener, right? Somehow, I got to learn your names. But in reality, you're a pair of Japanese *spies!"* He backed away from them, clearly alarmed. "You're tryin' to convince me and my friends to run away from New Orleans 'cause you want a clear shot for Tora, Tora, Tora to sabotage the Higgins Boat Factory! And now you've got me where you want me, 'cause Tora, Tora, Tora slipped me a drug that took away my vampiric super-powers!"

He slammed the door in their faces. Shogo heard the door being bolted from inside. "<Emiko,>" Shogo said, "<I think that our friend Jules has gone insane. He is like that Japanese soldier I saw in the documentary on the History Channel — he still thinks he is fighting World War Two! Really — an enemy called 'Tora, Tora, Tora'?>"

Emiko, never one to take "no" for an answer, pounded on the door, but to no avail. Despite several minutes of loud knocking, Jules refused to come back to the door. Shogo tried to convince his cousin to desist. They both saw him up above, peering fearfully at them from behind the curtain of the upstairs bedroom's window.

Finally, Emiko admitted temporary defeat and stopped knocking. "<We cannot abandon him, Shogo, no matter how crazy he might be now! There are still the lives of the others to consider, too — Doctor Landrieu and Maureen are also our friends. We must keep a careful watch on the Matter Master's movements. We will likely need to use our super-powers to confront him when he finally makes his move. I may be the best one to fight him — when I am Anime Girl, I am composed of electrons, and the Matter Master only has control over matter. I may be able to transform him into a cute cartoon figure and pull him with me into the world

of electromagnetic energy, the surging pulses of energy which make up the Internet, and then abandon him there. That would be one way to dispose of him!>"

"<That is a good plan, cousin. I, too, would like to battle the Matter Master...>"

"<No, Shogo, you must not! Your job should be only to supply me with your fan-boy batteries when I need them, so that I can power up and become Anime Girl. If you become Cutie-Scary Man and transform into one of your monstrous visages, it will be for naught — you are powerful, but you are too slow and clumsy to stay away from the Matter Master's hands. Should he lay his right hand upon you for more than a few seconds, he can transform you into a statue, a park bench, or a large serving of *beignet* fried donuts!>"

"<Shogo Fukuda is not afraid,>" he said firmly.

"<But perhaps Shogo Fukuda *should be* afraid,>" his cousin answered.

Nine

WILL *my plan to give Jules back his vampiric powers* ever *work?* Doodlebug thought despairingly. Thus far, his friend had proven virtually impenetrable to the power of suggestion.

Jules, dressed in his Hooded Terror costume (Doodlebug, Maureen, and Amos Landrieu were also wearing their World War Two-vintage costumes), stared with obvious confusion at the people milling around him in his living room. Some of them were lying upon phlebotomy tables and donating blood. One of them stared up at Jules and said, "Hey, dude, great costume! But, like, wasn't Halloween a month ago? And shouldn't you be dressed up as a vampire, anyway?"

Doodlebug could see that this quip and question made absolutely no sense to Jules and merely increased his confusion. Jules ignored what the man had said.

"Hey, Doodlebug," Jules whispered through his hood's mouth hole, "how come the guests about to go on tour are donatin' blood?"

"Remember what I told you?" Doodlebug whispered back to him. "These are all important government officials and defense contractors. They're donating blood because they want to make sure you stay a healthy vampire and that you're able to continue guarding the Higgins Boat Factory."

"But I don't even know where it is," Jules said.

"Right. It's, uh, supposed to be that way."

"And don't the officials and contractors figure I take in enough blood from Nazi saboteurs to get by?"

"Uh," Doodlebug said, "I, well, I think they realize that Tora, Tora, Tora has taken away your vampiric powers for the time being, so they figure you *can't* hunt down Nazi saboteurs. And they don't want you to get hungry."

"Oh, right. I get it. Thanks, little buddy."

Doodlebug could tell that Jules, as the Hooded Terror, was very confused, too, as to why he should be conducting a tour of the French Quarter for a group of government agents and war munitions industrialists. He had tried explaining to his friend that the whole purpose of having him do so was to entice Tora, Tora, Tora to show himself, but Jules hadn't fully accepted that explanation. *If only we weren't so desperate to return Jules's vampiric powers to him,* Doodlebug thought, *if only I didn't need to keep this masquerade going until Jules regains his confidence in his powers, I'd snap him out of his hypnotic trance and tell him the whole truth. We* are *trying to smoke out a Japanese enemy. But that enemy is Matsuba, Matter Master, not this imaginary Tora, Tora, Tora...*

As the Hooded Terror, Jules conducted his usual *Real* Vampires of New Orleans tour, Doodlebug noticed, but with a twist — rather than spouting made-up stories about vampires from the French colonial period, Jules told true stories of his and Doodlebug's real-life conflicts with Nazi saboteurs during World War Two. Along with pointing out and explaining the significance of various Vieux Carré historical landmarks, he also told the "government agents and war munitions industrialists" (actually honeymooners from Minnesota and New York, and tourists from Massachusetts and California — Doodlebug had lost track of the various places this tour group hailed from) war stories about his conflicts with the Austrian vampire, Count von Shrek, the Nazi Bader-Meinhoff Gang, and the real Tora, Tora, Tora, who had once tried to blow up the Higgins Boat Factory with a truckload of stolen dynamite.

As they walked through Jackson Square, heavily shadowed in the moonlight by the bulky edifices of the St. Louis Cathedral, the Cabildo, the Presbytère, and the Pontalba Apartments, Doodlebug noticed that Jules stopped talking with his tour group and stared at a figure at the far end of the square, a figure which sat behind a folding table next to the iron fence which surrounded the gardens and the equestrian statue of General Andrew Jackson. Doodlebug could barely see him through the wisps of fall fog which drifted through the square, but he saw that the figure wore an oddly tall hat, much like President Lincoln's famous stovepipe hat, but even taller.

Who could it be? Was he a Jackson Square busker of some kind? But Doodlebug didn't see any musical instrument case lying at the man's feet. A tarot card reader, perhaps? Doodlebug had no idea, but Jules was staring at the figure with such intensity that Doodlebug was tempted to walk across the square and ask the man who he was and what he was doing there. But then Jules shook his head as though he was clearing fog out of it, and he continued his spiel. The group resumed walking past the Presbytère and out of Jackson Square.

Doodlebug could sense his friend becoming more nervous and antsy by the minute. When the group finally reached the public access television studio (which Doodlebug had described as a "top secret televisionic test laboratory," since TV had only been in its very beginning stages during World War Two), Jules sent the group inside but signaled for his "super-hero friends" to stay outside with him.

"Guys," he said to the group, "there's something I didn't get a chance to tell y'all before I started conducting this important tour for all the industrialists and dignitaries. Before we left the house tonight, back when I was by myself, a pair of Jap spies paid me a visit. A young woman and a young guy. They tried to convince me and all of you to run away from New Orleans. I think they're the tip of a Jap circle of saboteurs, workin' with Tora, Tora, Tora— "

"Wait a minute," Maureen said. "Japanese spies? A girl and a young guy...?" Doodlebug saw Maureen stared at Jules with dawning understanding. "Would any of these spies be named Kenji, Shogo, or Emiko?"

"How the heck did you know?" Jules asked, astonished. "Yeah, that's absolutely right — the girl was named Emiko, and the guy was named Shogo! I stopped them from gettin' in our house, despite my bein' stripped of my vampire super-powers. Like I said, they want to chase us away from New Orleans so they'll have a clear shot at sabotogin' the Higgins Boat Factory. I think maybe they didn't take advantage of my loss of powers and just go ahead and kill me 'cause they're leavin' that chore for some big-time Jap assassin named Matter Master that Tora, Tora, Tora has ordered sicced on me. I think what we need to do now is split up. Me and Wondrous Woman will guard this secret televisionic test studio. Doodlebug and Doctor Supernatural, you guys go back to my house and guard it against those spies comin' back and infiltratin'. Knowing them sneaky Japs, they probably want to stick booby traps everywhere they can find a dark corner."

"Doodlebug," Maureen whispered desperately, "how do we handle this?"

"This Emiko and Shogo," Doodlebug whispered back, "they're your friends, right?"

"Yes! They're two of the superpowered Japanese *tarento* who helped us a few months back, right after Hurricane Antonia. The only reason they could possibly be in town is to help us again, this time against Matter Master!"

"In that case," Doodlebug whispered, "we've got to give them time to help us, and in case they can't do the job themselves, time to help Jules gain back his vampiric powers so he won't be completely at the mercy of Matter Master. In his normal form, he's too slow and clumsy to keep himself away from Matter Master's matter manipulating hands; he'd have better luck as a wolf or a bat. As much as I hate the thought of us splitting up when it sounds like Matter Master may've already reached New Orleans, I think we need to play along with Jules to keep this simulation of his World War Two activities feeling real to him."

He turned to Jules. "All right, Hooded Terror," he said, doing his best to hide the reluctance in his voice. "Doctor Supernatural and I will immediately head back to your house to guard it from the Japanese spies. Good luck to you and Wondrous Woman."

* * * * *

The Hooded Terror escorted Wondrous Woman into the top-secret televisionic test studio. He had split up the four of them the way he had with a very definite intention in mind. Despite his temporary loss of his vampiric powers, he was determined to protect Wondrous Woman. Even though she had super strength and a magic lasso which caused excruciating pain when wound around the body of any fool who would deign to tell her a lie, still he felt a powerful, primal need to be by her side and to protect her from all the forces of evil, even at the cost of his own undead existence.

They joined the assembled government dignitaries and war munitions industrialists inside the studio. The Hooded Terror glanced quickly around him. For a top-secret installation, this place seemed very lightly guarded — in fact, not guarded at all. The only new faces he could see belonged to technicians working the top-secret televisionic equipment. Maybe all the guards were on secret surveillance, hidden behind two-way bullet-proof glass?

The Hooded Terror remembered something disconcerting from his leisure-time reading. In *Captain America Comics* #1, a Nazi saboteur penetrated the secret installation which housed Operation: Rebirth and shot and killed Professor Reinstein just after he used his equipment and chemicals to transform skinny Steve Rogers into the mighty Captain America. The Hooded Terror silently prayed that the security here was more fool-proof than it had been at the site of Operation: Rebirth. Yes, that had just been a story in a comic book. Still, thinking about it gave him the willies.

Wondrous Woman motioned for him to sit down in the audience. Then she took her place on the studio floor in front of the top-secret televisionic test equipment. The Hooded Terror hadn't realized that she would be the one leading the demonstration for the assembled dignitaries.

"Tonight," Wondrous Woman said, "Morganna the Marvelous will present for your dismayed and deranged enjoyment an oldy-but-stinky called *Dracula vs. Frankenstein.*"

Ah-ha — 'Morganna the Marvelous' must be Wondrous Woman's code name while she's workin' on this top-secret televisionic project, the Hooded Terror thought.

"But first," Wondrous Woman said, "we get to find out who gets sent down to the Self-Abasement Basement. For those of you who are unfamiliar with my show, the Self-Abasement Basement is where I send two unlucky audience members who are stuck in the basement, on camera, and who can't come out again until they manage to make the audience laugh by making an even funnier quip about the rotten movie than I can. Everybody check beneath your seats. You'll find a number stuck to the bottom of your chair. I'm going to draw two numbers from the lottery mixer, and whoever's numbers I pull out gets sent down."

The Hooded Terror frowned. This whole procedure seemed very strange for a test demonstration of top-secret televisionic equipment. But he figured he needed to play along with Wondrous Woman, just as all of the assembled dignitaries were doing. He was certain this activity must be absolutely vital to the war effort. He felt beneath his seat for the hidden number. His fingers felt a piece of paper. He grabbed it. His number was 29.

On stage, Wondrous Woman was cranking the handle of a mesh barrel which was partially filled with slips of paper. Then she stopped cranking and opened the hatch on the barrel's side. She pulled out two pieces of paper. The Hooded Terror watched an expression of surprise blossom on her pretty face. (*Yes, she certainly is pretty,* the Hooded Terror thought; *if only I thought I'd have a chance with her, I'd ask her out on a date... but a fabulous super-heroine like her would never consent to a romantic liaison with a vampire like me...)*

"Big shocker tonight," Wondrous Woman said, holding the two pieces of paper over her head so that all the audience members could see the two numbers. "For the first time ever on *The Morganna the Marvelous Show,* I've picked two consecutive numbers! Will Numbers 16 and 17 please come up on stage?"

The two government agents or industrialists who headed for the stage appeared oddly familiar to Jules. The woman, not so much; she had slathered herself in pancake makeup and appeared to be wearing a blonde wig. But the Negro... gosh darn it, the Hooded Terror just *knew* he knew that Negro from *somewhere.* Who could forget a character like that, with his lazy eye? *He must be the blonde lady's man servant,* the Hooded Terror thought. Weirdly enough, Wondrous Woman also seemed to recognize the Negro.

"Erato!" Wondrous Woman said to the Negro, clapping him heartily on the shoulder. "I'm so *glad* to see you decided to use that free pass Jules and I gave you!"

"Hello, Ms. Maureen," the Negro said in a friendly tone. How bizarre that a famous super-heroine like Wondrous Woman would be friendly with a common Negro! But the Hooded Terror wiped his forehead with a sense of distress. Where did he know the name "Erato" from...?

"Okay, you two unlucky folks," Wondrous Woman said, "follow me down to the Self-Abasement Basement! Audience, you can watch all the wacky goings-on on the TV monitors mounted on the wall behind the stage."

The three of them disappeared through a doorway. A minute and a half later, the Hooded Terror saw them reappear on the televisionic monitors, and in *full color!* What would modern technology come up with next?

"Okay, you two crazy kids," Wondrous Woman said from the televisionic screens, "here's the deal. You've got about two dozen wacky costumes to choose from. You both pick one out, strip down to your undies — remember, this is the Self-Abasement Basement! — and then redress in the ridiculous costume of your choice. Then you have one minute in which to make the audience upstairs laugh. I'll be able to tell if they're laughing by watching that TV monitor there. If you can't manage to get them howling with laughter in under a minute — and your joke or quip has to have something to do with tonight's movie — you're stuck down here for the remainder of the show!"

The Negro named Erato began unbuttoning his shirt and unbuckling his belt. But the Hooded Terror could see that the blonde woman was doing something very odd, very odd indeed... she had taken a piece of white chalk out of her purse and was drawing something on the floor. Something really *big,* which the Hooded Terror couldn't see on the televisionic screens. But whatever she was drawing on the floor required the woman to walk around the Negro and Wondrous Woman.

The Hooded Terror started to sweat. Something wasn't right here. Something was very, very *wrong...*

The woman in the blonde wig in the basement chanted something in a language the Hooded Terror had never heard before. Then she stood back and cackled. "*Ha!* Morganna the Marvelous — or should I call you Maureen Remoulade? — I've trapped you like a fly on fly paper! While you were watching your friend strip down to his undies, I drew a *mystical pentagram* around the two of you, and I chanted an ancient Sumerian captivity spell! Until that pentagram is broken, neither of you is going *anywhere!* And Maureen, I'm going to phone Matter Master right now, and he's going to come here and remove your rotten head from Flora

Ann's torso!"

"Now I know where I know you from!" Wondrous Woman cried. "You're one of the High Krewe's brats, aren't you? And you're wearing makeup and a wig so you wouldn't appear partially invisible on TV!"

The Hooded Terror had seen and heard enough. The beauteous Wondrous Woman was in deadly danger! He leaped up from his chair, ran through the studio's interior door, and speed-waddled his way down the stairs.

There they were, the three of them. What had that terrible blonde-wigged woman said about the pentagram? Something about as long as it remained unbroken, the other two would remain trapped inside it? Well then, he would have to break it!

Before the blonde-wigged woman could do or say a thing, the Hooded Terror charged to the pentagram and rubbed out a portion of it with his shoe. Then he grabbed Wondrous Woman and yanked her out of the pentagram, pulling her towards the stairs.

He heard the blonde-wigged woman ranting and raving behind them. "Damn you! *Damn you,* Jules Duchon! I *had* her! But you had to come and ruin *everything!* I can't fight both of you, so you can escape us for now... but not for long!"

Panting with exertion (*I really need to get some exercise, I've somehow gotten horribly out of shape,* he thought), the Hooded Terror paused for a second in the doorway of the televisionic studio to watch what was transpiring in the basement.

"All right," the blonde-wigged woman said to the camera. "So I'm supposed to make everybody *laugh?* And my gag's supposed to have something to do with *Dracula vs. Frankenstein?* How about *this,* you bunch of idiots?" She bent Erato's head to the side and savagely bit his neck. Blood gushed out of the wound, staining the woman's dress and thoroughly soaking her blonde wig. Then the strange woman began hungrily lapping up the blood and sucking more out of Erato's neck.

She was a *vampire!*

Now it was Wondrous Woman's turn to yank on his arm. "Jules — uh, I mean Hooded Terror," she stuttered, "we've got to get *out of here!* That skinny bitch almost trapped me! If you hadn't come down to save me, I would've been a sitting target for Matter Master!"

Ten

HIRO Matsuba, the Matter Master, had expected to capture Maureen Remoulade as she exited her studio at 12:35 A.M., after the conclusion of her show. He had planned to turn her into a plastic mannequin of herself, take her back to the High Krewe's compound, and have the High Krewe's servants, Otranto and Hecht, saw the mannequin into pieces — legs, arms, torso, and head. Matsuba would then transform the torso and limbs back into their original states, as vampire flesh. The servants would then re-attach the legs, arms, and torso to the High Krewe's women who lay dormant in comas, reviving them. As for what the High Krewe would do with Maureen Remoulade's plastic head...? Well, that was their business, he thought.

Being a punctilious sort of assassin, the Matter Master had arrived an hour early to stake out the studio, wanting to leave nothing to chance. Yet as he watched the front of the public access TV studio from the shadows beneath the Pontchartrain Expressway overpass, it appeared as though his carefully considered time table might have been disrupted. It was only 11:37 P.M., and the audience members were already filing out of the studio, nearly an hour earlier than they should have been.

He listened to some of their chatter:

"Are you sure you don't want to stay for the rest of the movie?" one woman asked her male companion.

"Naww," the man replied. "Maureen the Marvelous took a powder, so as far as I'm concerned, the show's over. Anyway, wasn't that one hellavah great special effects job down in the Self-Abasement Basement? I could've sworn that was *real blood* spurting out of that black dude's neck."

Something has gone wrong, Hiro Matsuba thought. *I must enter the studio to learn what has happened.*

He strode from beneath the overpass and crossed the street to the studio. One of the departing audience members noticed that Matsuba was heading in the opposite direction of everyone else. "Hey, buddy, you going in there to watch the rest of *Dracula vs. Frankenstein* on the monitors?"

"No." Matsuba pushed past him, in no mood to tarry with trivialities.

"Well, you won't get to see Morganna the Marvelous, if you're looking for her autograph," the man called after him. "She flew outta here like a dragon was on her tail."

Matsuba pushed his way through the glass doors which led into the studio complex. *What could have happened?* he thought. *For what possible reason could the Remoulade woman have fled her own hosting duties an hour early?*

He learned a major part of the answer as soon as he entered the particular studio from which *The Morganna the Marvelous Show* had been broadcast. On the studio's monitors, he saw a young woman who he recognized as belonging to the High Krewe of Vlad Tepes; she was drinking the blood of a black man down in the basement level beneath the studio.

Matsuba felt fury begin to boil in his chest. "<That little fool!>" he muttered angrily to himself in Japanese. "<How dare she come here and cause my target to flee? What could she have been thinking?>"

He marched purposefully down the stairs, determined to severely chastise the young woman. It was unfortunate that she was a member of the High Krewe, and thus one of his clients; otherwise, she would receive far worse than a harsh chastisement. He would have transformed her into a beanbag chair.

When he reached the basement, he saw that the black man's eyes were still partially open, although his neck was bent at a most uncomfortable angle so that the young vampiress could feed. The black man saw Matsuba. He haltingly reached for him, a pathetically weak gesture. Were Matsuba's heart not so hardened from more than twenty years working as a super-powered assassin, he might have felt pity for the man. "Hel... help me..." the man gasped.

In case this scenario in the basement had been broadcast, Matsuba wanted there to be no chance of the broadcast continuing after his arrival. He did not want what he would say to the female vampire to be overheard by several thousand people, one of whom might be Jules Duchon. He strode to the camera which was focused on the vampiress and her victim and touched it with his right hand. Green energy arced from his hand into the camera. This energy was a form of stored solar energy, changed within his body by Matsuba's unique physiology into the transformative energy which glowed green. The camera immediately turned to stone. Its increased weight badly bent its tripod, and the camera fell to the floor and broke into five stone chunks.

The noise caused the vampiress to stop her feeding and look up at Matsuba. "Who are you?" she hissed.

"I am Hiro Matsuba, the Matter Master, the assassin your Triumvirate procured to eliminate Jules Duchon and his friends and to retrieve the stolen body parts. I would have done the latter tonight had you not interfered, foolish female." He stared down at the floor, where he had noticed a pentagram with one of its sides partially rubbed out. "Am I correct in surmising that you attempted to trap Maureen Remoulade in a Sumerian capture pentagram? I am familiar with it; it is a widely-known ancient vampiric spell."

"Yes, that's *exactly* what I wanted to do!" the vampiress said. She was quite a mess, Matsuba noticed. Blood dripped down her chin, and it had become spattered on her dress and what he presumed was a wig. "I wanted to *help you,* Matter Master! If Jules Duchon hadn't rubbed out part of my pentagram, I could've kept Maureen trapped inside it, called you, and had you come here and turn her into an overstuffed easy chair, or something..."

She cringed. Matsuba could tell that the enormity of her mistake was beginning to become apparent to her.

"You... you aren't going to do anything *awful* to me, are you?" she sputtered fearfully.

"You have roused my prey. You have made both Maureen Remoulade and Jules Duchon aware that they are being hunted. Ordinarily, I would slay you right now. But because you are a client, I will send you back to your compound with stern instructions *never* to emerge until I have accomplished my assignment. Do you understand?"

"Yes... yes, I understand..."

"Good," Matsuba said. He eyed the black man. "I shall have to dispose of this person. He has seen and heard too much. I believe I shall transform him into a plastic mannequin."

"You don't know who this is?" the vampiress asked.

"No. Would I have any reason to?"

"Well, it's just that I thought he might be on your list of targets. You're targeting all of Jules Duchon's family and friends, right? This man's name is Erato. Maureen Remoulade is very chummy with him, and I'll bet Jules Duchon is, too."

"This is true?"

The vampiress smiled, revealing blood-covered teeth. "If I'm lyin', I'm dyin'..."

Erato, crumpled on the floor, looked weakly up at Hiro Matsuba. “Wha... what are you gonna do to me, man?”

“Use you as bait,” Matsuba said. With that, he stepped inside the broken pentagram and knelt down next to Erato, then placed his right hand on Erato’s bloody shoulder. Green energy arced from the Japanese assassin’s hand into Erato’s body, and he was transformed into a plastic version of himself, spattered with painted-on blood and wearing plastic, molded-on clothes.

Then Matsuba slung the plastic mannequin over his shoulder — it was hinged at the waist — and pondered the long trek back to his rented cargo van, with which he would transport the plastic man back to the compound of the High Krewe of Vlad Tepes.

Eleven

THE Hooded Terror and Wondrous Woman didn't stop running until they reached a dark alleyway within the bounds of the Iberville Public Housing Project. The Hooded Terror glanced at the red-brick apartment buildings which surrounded him. "Nice... nice places Roosevelt's WPA has put up," he huffed, leaning over with his hands on his knees and trying to catch his breath. "Might even have runnin' water in the bathroom and kitchen. You think — you think we lost that Nazi vampire woman? Sure was a shame what she did to that poor Negro..."

"Hooded Terror," Wondrous Woman said, "you'd feel a whole lot *worse* if you knew who that Negro actually was."

The Hooded Terror was confused. "Why do you say that, Wondrous Woman?"

"Oh, Jules — uh, I mean, Hooded Terror — you've got *no darned idea* how *much* I want to explain. But Doodlebug told me I'd better not pull anything like that."

"Oh... uh, okay, I guess. Usually my little buddy has a pretty good reason for the stuff he says."

Maybe we got us ten minutes of quiet, the Hooded Terror thought. *Maybe five minutes, maybe four. But with Tora, Tora, Tora still on the loose, his pack of Jap saboteurs after us, and this new Jap assassin Matter Master in the mix, too, I'd better take whatever chance I've got to practice gettin' my vampire super-powers back. Doodlebug said Tora, Tora,*

Tora's drug might wear off at any time. Now's as good a time as any to test that notion, I figure.

"Wondrous Woman," he said, "I gotta ask you to look away from me for a minute or two. While we got us this little respite here, I wanna see if Tora, Tora, Tora's drug has worn off. I wanna see if I can transform into a wolf again."

"*Now* you're talking, Hooded Terror!" Wondrous Woman said, clearly relieved. "If you can transform into a wolf, then I can have Doodlebug unhypno — I mean, then we'll know for sure that Tora, Tora, Tora's drug was just temporary. I'll not only turn in the other direction, but I'll even put my hands over my eyes, okay, Hooded Terror?"

"Sure, fine." The Hooded Terror took off his hood and his cape, folded them reverently, and placed them carefully on the ground (which he noticed was covered with shards of broken beer bottles; he kicked them to the side with his foot). He was less careful with his shirt, pants, socks, and underwear; he just dumped them on top of his hood and cape. When his full naked glory was revealed beneath the moon (*Man oh man, I gotta go on a diet and hit the gym regularly — look at that big, pasty gut I got on me — how did I get so fat recently?*), the Hooded Terror concentrated with all his might on fur, paws, pointed, perky ears, and a long snout crowned with a black, wet nose.

He both saw and felt a gray, murky mist surrounding him. He was doing it! He was able to do it again! He was shedding a portion of his mass and transforming into a wolf!

No longer able to stand on his hind legs, the Hooded Terror bent over and landed on all four paws. He stared up at the moon and howled with triumph.

He saw that Wondrous Woman had uncovered her eyes and turned around to face him. "Oh, Jules! — I mean, uh, oh, Hooded Terror! You've *done* it! You've gotten your vampiric powers back!"

She bounded over to him and began petting his head and back. The

Hooded Terror decided to take a liberty he would never dare take while in human form. He jumped up, placed his paws on Wondrous Woman's curvaceous bosom, and licked her all over her face.

She let him do it. He briefly considered humping her leg in addition, but then he figured that would be going too far.

* * * * *

Hiro Matsuba knocked angrily on the door of Georges Bestoff's office. "Come," Besthoff said from inside. When Matsuba entered, Besthoff looked up from his desk. "You appear angry, sir. Has anything gone awry?"

"*Everything* has gone awry!" Matsuba snarled. "Your idiot female, Pearl, inadvertently tipped off Jules Duchon and Maureen Remoulade that they are being hunted and that you have ordered their assassination. They fled from Remoulade's television studio. By now, they are likely on the road to Baton Rouge, Lafayette, or even Lake Charles — anywhere they could transport coffins to before sunrise. Now that they have likely fled to another city, it could take me weeks, even months to locate them again! My only consolation is that I captured one of their friends, a black man named Erato."

Besthoff appeared lost in thought for a moment. "A hostage? That may work to our advantage. Possibly we could lure them both back to New Orleans, assuming they have fled the city, as you believe they have. We could place ads in newspapers in Baton Rouge, Lafayette, and Lake Charles to the effect that we have captured one of their friends. We could have radio ads broadcast with the same message. I could have Gregory Krauss, our resident computer expert, track down their email addresses, assuming they each have one. Somehow, they would get the message that we are holding this friend of theirs." Matsuba saw Besthoff's eyes light up with a new idea. "If one hostage would be a lure, how much better *two?* Rory Richelieu does not yet know that he has been included in the manhunt or in the High Krewe's vendetta. I know the perfect way to get him to come here, to this very compound. I shall phone him and tell him that due to various financial irregularities the Triumvirate have uncovered on his part, we are putting his institute into receivership. This is a lie, of course, but he will want to come here to clear his name with us and avoid losing his institute. When he arrives here, you could transform him into something inert — a nice coffee table, perhaps — and we could include in the advertisements (in carefully couched language, of course) and email messages to Duchon and Remoulade that in addition to capturing the black man, we have captured their closest friend, Doodlebug!"

Matsuba smiled. He liked this idea. He liked it very much. But he decided he could make it even better. "Why should I not capture *all* of Duchon's and Remoulade's friends and hold them hostage? I could immobilize each of them. Then our two primary targets would take the grave risk to come here for certain!"

* * * * *

Rory "Doodlebug" Richelieu's smart phone rang with his incoming call ring tone — the first few bars of "Forget Your Troubles, C'mon, Get Happy." He squirmed on the sofa in Jules's living room and dug the phone out of the pocket on the pants of his Doodlebug super-hero uniform (life was so much more convenient when he could carry a purse — he could hardly wait for the night this crisis was over with and he could become a woman again, not a pubescent boy).

He checked the screen to see where the call was coming from. The owner's identity was blocked; the screen read, "Unknown Caller." He answered the phone. "Yes? This is Rory Richelieu. To whom am I speaking?"

He recognized the voice immediately. "Ms. Richelieu, this is Georges Besthoff. I must speak to you as soon as possible, and in person. Please arrange a flight to New Orleans at your earliest convenience."

Doodlebug's breath caught in his throat. "What — what is this all about, Mr. Besthoff?"

"The other members of the Triumvirate and I have uncovered evidence of gross financial irregularities on your part. Unless you come before us and explain these irregularities as soon as possible, we will be forced to place your institute into receivership."

"I... I see," Doodlebug said. He had to stall for time, until he could learn what the Triumvirate's true intentions toward him were. Did they actually intend to put his institute into receivership? Or was that threat just bait to get him to come to their compound to be killed? "Oh, uh, yes, Mr. Besthoff, I'll schedule a flight to New Orleans immediately. Let me call you back in just a few minutes, once I've been able to book a flight, and I'll tell you when I'm coming in."

"That will be acceptable. Good night, Ms. Richelieu. I look forward to hearing back from you shortly."

Doodlebug was tormented by indecision. He decided the best thing to do was to play along with them for now and use whatever time he could gain to see Johann Straussman, the High Krewe's butler, who was secretly Jules's and Maureen's informant of the Triumvirate's malignant plans. Straussman would be able to tell him what the true intentions of the Triumvirate towards Rory Richelieu were.

He waited a few minutes, then looked up the High Krewe's main telephone number in an old phone book which Maureen still kept in the house. Hecht, one of the servants, answered the phone. "Yes, I will connect you to Master Besthoff, Ms. Richelieu," he said. "He has been expecting your call."

A moment later, Bestoff's voice came on the line. "This is Besthoff, Ms. Richelieu. When will you be arriving?"

"I was able to book a flight to New Orleans for tomorrow evening. I should be arriving at the airport around 2 A.M., New Orleans time. So, figuring the time it takes to collect my luggage and hire a cab, then drive to your compound, I should arrive at about 3:45 A.M."

"We will be awaiting you, Ms. Richelieu. We have much to discuss. And you had better have some convincing explanations, if you want to keep your institute."

"I'm sure I'll be able to clear up whatever the problems are, Mr. Besthoff."

"Pray that you can, Ms. Richelieu."

Then Besthoff hung up the phone.

I'll have to go see Straussman tonight, Doodlebug thought. *Surreptitiously. Well, there's no reason to remain the* ***1940s*** *version of Rory Richelieu any longer. I might as well transform into the twenty-first century version — that way, Straussman will recognize me immediately.*

Doodlebug, now in his standard form as a shapely young woman, cautiously walked through the thick woods which lay between Metairie Road and the compound of the High Krewe of Vlad Tepes. Dry leaves crunched underfoot. He carried a backpack with him. When he reached the edge of the woods closest to the ten-foot high brick wall which surrounded the compound, he scanned the top of the wall for the security cameras. He spotted four of them; each slowly swept a field of vision, back and forth, back and forth.

He selected a stretch of woods directly between two of the cameras. In the shelter of the darkness provided by the small forest, he tied his hair back in a bun and stripped off his watch, bracelets, rings, blouse, pants, socks, and panties. He folded them neatly and placed them in his backpack.

Then he waited for the five second stretch when neither camera in its mechanical back-and-forth sweeping was focused on his section of woods. As soon as this occurred, he hurled the backpack over the wall. It landed with a reassuringly muted thud on the grass on the far side.

Now Doodlebug concentrated on black wings, tall, pointed ears, and an ugly rodent's face. He smelled the scent of his own skin and perfume boiling away as he sent the greater portion of his mass through the null dimension into the shelter of his own coffin, where it would reside as gray, jelly-like proto-mass until he transformed back into a young woman.

He stretched his wings and waited for the cameras to again sweep away from his section of the woods. It felt good to be a bat again; he would have to remember to do this more often. Then he took flight. It was a brief flight, only long enough to get him silently over the wall. He landed next to his backpack, transformed back into his standard womanly shape, and quickly re-dressed.

Thank Varney, Straussman's room in the main compound building has an outside door, he thought. *With any luck, I'll be admitted, ask my questions, and then leave without anyone other than Straussman being the wiser.*

The windows of Straussman's room, curtained with a heavy material, were mostly dark. Just a tiny bit of illumination escaped through the seams of the curtains; it might be a candle or night-light, Doodlebug conjectured. There was a possibility Straussman might not be in his room. He could be performing his duties somewhere in the compound. Or, monk-like (Doodlebug knew Straussman led an almost monastic existence), he might be lying on the simple cot which held his coffin, reading Elizabethan poetry by candlelight.

He knocked softly on the door, not wanting to alert anyone but Straussman, assuming the butler was in his room. Doodlebug appeared to be fortunate — the door opened for him.

He entered the small room. His eyes were momentarily dazzled by the single uncovered light bulb, which was much brighter than he had first supposed.

As soon as he was fully inside, the door slammed shut behind him and two powerful sets of hands grabbed his upper arms.

"What—?" he cried. This wasn't the welcome he'd been expecting.

"Thank you, Hecht and Otranto," a voice said from the shadows. Doodlebug recognized the voice as belonging to Georges Besthoff. As soon as his vision adjusted to the bright light, he saw the lead member of the Triumvirate, gloating with a broad smile on his face. "Gentlemen, please hold him until Hiro Matsuba comes."

"Hiro Matsuba?" Doodlebug asked, struggling against the hands holding him. He knew his struggles were futile; each of the vampires who held him was at least as strong as he was. "You mean the Matter Master? The assassin you've assigned to kill Jules?"

"Hold that pose just a few minutes longer, gentlemen and lady," Besthoff said. He turned to another figure standing in the shadows, a young woman. Doodlebug recognized her as Pearl, one of the High Krewe's young vampiresses. "Pearl, would you be a dear and fetch Mr. Matsuba for me?"

"With *pleasure,* Mr. Besthoff!" Pearl said. She exited through the door which led into a hallway of the main compound building.

Besthoff turned back to Doodlebug. "Now, Ms. Richelieu, in the few moments left to you, I assume you have some questions you would like to have answered. Since answering them will not harm me in the least, and may indeed provide me some amusement, I will deign to answer whatever questions I can."

"How did you know I would be here tonight, in this room?"

"Oh, I didn't. Not for certain. Before I placed the call to you, I assumed there was a possibility you might have already arrived in New Orleans to attempt to assist your friends. Thus, I asked my colleague, Gregory Krauss, to put his computer expertise to work. As soon as you answered your cell phone, Krauss's computer, from which I phoned you — what marvelous inventions this twenty-first century has provided us! — it inserted a virus across the cellular connection, which utilized your own phone's GPS to reveal your precise location. Which was in the French Quarter of New Orleans. So it was only prudent to also assume that, having told me to expect you tomorrow night, you might come here this evening, secretly, in hopes of talking with Johann Straussman."

"Where is Straussman?"

Besthoff chuckled. It was an ugly sound, not humorous at all. "Oh, Mr. Straussman is occupying the library. As an end table. He makes a rather handsome piece of furniture. I believe I shall have Mr. Matsuba transform you into a coffee table. That way, our library can have a matched French Provincial suite."

"Why, Besthoff? Why did you do this to your own servant, loyal to you for centuries?"

"Oh, I suppose Mr. Straussman *was* loyal for many centuries," Besthoff said. "But for the past three years, he has been most *disloyal.* He conspired with you and your friends, Dr. Amos Landrieu and Jules Duchon, to kidnap and butcher three of my blood-children. Wouldn't you say that is the height of disloyalty?"

Doodlebug knew the answer to his next question, but he needed to know whether Besthoff knew it. The consequences of Besthoff knowing the answer to this next question quivered Rory Richelieu's soul. "Why in Varney's name would Johann Straussman bother to conspire with Jules and Amos, particularly to carry out something so dastardly and grisly?"

Besthoff smiled again. "Oh, Ms. Richelieu, now you are being too clever by half. You know *exactly* why Mr. Straussman conspired with you and your friends. Maureen Remoulade had been banished by Malice X, leader of that noxious pack of black vampires, to the netherworld. You conducted a mystical ceremony which apparently only was able to retrieve Ms. Remoulade's head from the residue of her ashes. Our Straussman is Ms. Remoulade's blood-father. He loves her very deeply; at one time, he intended her for his own consort. He conspired with the three of you to butcher my three blood-children — his blood-*sisters,* I might add — so that Dr. Amos Landrieu could obtain a torso and sets of arms and legs for Ms. Remoulade's use. The four of you are guilty of body snatching and butchery. All of you will be put to death by being made inert matter forever, until this house crumbles and termites eat you in some distant epoch."

"What... what do you intend to do with Maureen?"

"Ms. Remoulade? She will die with the rest of you. But we of the Triumvirate will make full use of her corpse. Her torso shall be returned to Flora Ann. Her legs shall be returned to Victoria. Her arms shall be returned to Alexandra. As for her head? Oh, I don't know... perhaps I shall have Mr. Matsuba transform it into a lovely glass knickknack which I will display upon my favorite coffee table... which will be you, Ms. Richelieu, of course."

Just then the door opened. An imposing looking middle-aged Japanese man, arms taut with well-defined musculature, entered the room.

"Mr. Matsuba?" Besthoff said. "Please allow me to introduce Ms. Rory Richelieu. If I may be so bold as to guide your hand, I would truly appreciate it if you could change the charming lady into a coffee table which matches Mr. Straussman's end table."

"Of course, Mr. Besthoff," Matsuba replied. "Your pleasure is my pleasure."

"Hecht and Otranto, hold her tightly," Besthoff said. "Mr. Matsuba has assured me his energy discharge will not affect you in any way."

Doodlebug made a last ditch effort to spring free, but the two vampires were too strong for him. Matsuba held his right hand against Doodlebug's chest. The Japanese man began glowing a bright green color. Then a surge of green energy arced from his fingertips into Doodlebug's chest.

Doodlebug felt his body turning wooden. Then everything went black...

* * * * *

The Hooded Terror lurched forward in Wondrous Woman's bedroom and caught himself from falling by hanging onto the door. When his mind cleared of its sudden fog, he wasn't the Hooded Terror anymore. He was just plain Jules Duchon.

"Hooded Terror?" Maureen asked. She had been stuffing a few personal care items into a small suitcase. "Are you feeling all right? What happened just now?"

"I ain't the Hooded Terror no more," Jules said. "I don't think I'm back in the 1940s any longer. I know I'm in the right now."

"But — but Doodlebug had hypnotized you— "

"I know. He hypnotized me to go back to a time when I believed I could get my lost vampire powers back, and since I believed, I got them back. But now *I'm* back... and since Doodlebug wasn't here to snap me outta his hypnosis, that can only mean one thing."

"Whu-what, Jules?"

"My little buddy is dead."

"Oh, Varney... don't say something like that...!"

"I gotta. It's the truth. It's the only possible explanation for what just happened. Go stick your stuff in the car, Maureen. We don't have more than a few hours left before sunrise. I'll pack up the dirt that's lying around our bed into pillow cases and carry it down to the Cadillac's trunk. That's where we're gonna be sleepin', hon... in an underground parking garage somewheres downtown. At least as long as Matter Master is on the loose.

"And you can bet on this, hon — I'm gonna get that Jap bastard for rubbin' out Doodlebug. I don't care if he's as powerful as Godzilla... I'm gonna get him."

Twelve

JULES selected one of the subterranean parking garages located in the French Quarter, the highest part of town and thus the only district which allowed for underground structures. He and Maureen slept very uncomfortably in the Cadillac's massive trunk, which Jules had had fitted with an interior pull-release years before, in case of just such an emergency as this (then, the emergency had been his need to escape the clutches of Malice X).

The next night, he and Maureen awoke, both with severe kinks in their necks. They each had to perform stretching exercises within the otherwise empty lowest level of the parking garage to work out the painful neck muscle spasms (for Jules, any type of exercise verged on the implausible, but he did those exercises at Maureen's insistence, nonetheless).

"Where do we go now, Jules? Do we drive to Lake Charles tonight and hide out there?"

Jules shook his head, even though his neck was still sore. "Hell, no," he said angrily. "I ain't runnin' nowheres. This ain't like when Malice X burned down my house and I ran to Baton Rouge like a dog with its tail between its legs. I learned my lesson when that crumb killed you with a stake through the heart. You don't leave your loved ones behind. Doodlebug may be gone, but there's still Doc, my mom, and you that that lousy bum Matter Master's gunnin' for. And now our pals Emiko and Shogo are somehow mixed up in this, too. I gotta keep your all's safety in mind. I ain't running off no place until I'm sure that guy's six feet under."

"But Kenji said that Matter Master's more powerful all by himself than the entire Acme Talent Peerless Proficiencies Trio put together! How do you mean to kill him?"

"I may not have the answer. But I'll bet Super-Genius Jules does."

"Super-Genius Jules?" Maureen said. "But the last we saw of him, three months ago, he was in a boat, heading out for deep water. Wouldn't he still be on the bottom of the ocean, mulling over Einstein's Theory of Relativity or something like that?"

"He ain't on the bottom of the Gulf of Mexico no more," Jules said. "He only stayed there long enough to make sure he wouldn't transform back into a smaller version of 'Regular Jules' when the effects of Emiko's blood wore off on me. Emiko told me he's in the French Quarter, in Jackson Square, just a few blocks from here. He's workin' as a fortune teller, I guess usin' his genius at sizin' people up to predict what they're gonna do next. She told me after I'd been hypnotized to think I was the Hooded Terror, but I remember the conversation."

"You think Super-Genius Jules will be willing to help us?" Maureen asked.

"He don't have no reason on Earth to help me. But since he's really just an ex-part of me, he loves Maureen Duchon with all his heart. Even if he won't help me, he'll wanna do all he can to help *you*."

Despite the darkness, Maureen thought she saw Super-Genius Jules sitting behind a card table next to the fence surrounding the Jackson Square garden and equestrian statue of General Andrew Jackson.

"There he is," Jules whispered to her when they reached the edge of Jackson Square closest to the Presbytère. "He's that funky-lookin' dude sittin' over there by the fence. The one with the Abe Lincoln hat. Guess the hat covers up his freakishly tall head."

"That's him, all right," Maureen whispered back to him. "I'd recognize him anywhere. Aside from his weird, tall forehead, he looks like a skinny, 180-pound version of you."

"Here's what I want you to do. You go over to him first, okay? I'll listen in on the conversation from here, but I'll stick to the shadows. He'll be more likely to talk to you alone, at least at first. If I just walk up to him outta the blue, he'll think I wanna re-absorb him into me or somethin'. He'd probably run, and with them skinny, muscular legs of his, he's a lot faster than either of us. Especially me."

"Okay, Jules. You stay here for right now, and I'll go talk with him."

What should I call him? Maureen thought. *'Super-Genius Jules'? 'Jules Number Two'? 'Big Head Jules'? Or just plain 'Jules'? I think I'll stick with just plain 'Jules'...*

Maureen felt strange approaching this man, this weird, fun house mirror reflection of her husband. The last time she'd seen him had been three months ago, when she and Kenji Tezuka had stood helplessly on the ruined dock near the Rigolets in New Orleans East, and Super-Genius Jules had made his escape to the Gulf in the only undamaged boat in the harbor. He'd made a loving gesture toward her then — he'd called out to her the ingredients for a counter-agent which would neutralize the effects of Kenji's blood in her system and allow her to enjoy intimate relations with her husband once again. That had been a completely unselfish gesture, since Super-Genius Jules would never be able to benefit from it. Didn't that mean that he felt some sort of love for her?

When she approached his table, she saw what the blueish glow in his hands was. He was staring down at a reading tablet, reading some book or article at incredible speed, flipping the electronic pages as almost quickly as his fingers could move.

She stood before his table and cleared her throat. "Hello, Jules," she said.

Super-Genius Jules looked up. His face registered surprise for less than half a second. "Maureen," he said. "I anticipated that you might come. Emiko and Shogo told you I was here, did they not?"

"They actually told Jules — uh, *my* Jules."

"I see." He peered into the shadows surrounding the square. "That is him standing over there, is it not?"

"Yes. He didn't want to scare you."

"I would not have been frightened had he come with you. I realize that you both only seek information and advice. Emiko and Shogo explained to me that you are both being hunted by Hiro Matsuba, the Matter Master of Japan, a deadly assassin for hire. Your family and friends are also being hunted. I assume you wish to ask me what weaknesses the Matter Master suffers from, so that you may have some chance of defeating or killing him before he kills you."

"Uh, yeah, that's exactly right," Maureen said. *Yup, he's not called 'Super-Genius Jules' for nothing,* she thought.

"I have watched one of his anime movies, the one which you broadcast on your public access television show. Assuming that this anime movie was accurate in portraying his abilities and fighting style, I have determined the following. When he is in his flesh and blood form, he has nearly all the vulnerabilities of a standard human being. Were either of you a marksman, you could kill him from long-distance with a sniper's rifle, since he must be close enough to touch you with his right hand to transform you into inert matter. However, there are several difficulties with using a sniper's rifle. First of all, neither you nor standard Jules is an expert marksman; I believe that your Jules has never fired a rifle, although he has fired a crossbow. Second of all, you would need to catch him unawares. I believe this to be statistically almost impossible. He is stealthy, and he is hunting you. You could stake out a sniper's position in the woods adjacent to the High Krewe's compound and wait for his car to emerge from behind the ten-foot-tall brick walls, but then you would need to hit him through tinted glass and in a moving vehicle. The likelihood of either of you being able to accomplish this feat is extremely unlikely and would require at least three months' worth of sniper's training, time which you do not have.

"There is a third disadvantage to trying to kill him with a gun or any other projectile weapon. If he has at least three seconds' notice of your presence and sees you carrying such a weapon, he can utilize his powers on himself. He is capable, according to the anime film, of transforming his epidermis into a jointed set of titanium armor, armor which cannot be penetrated by anything less than an artillery shell. Ordinary bullets will simply bounce off him. You could attempt to use a machete to slice off his right hand, but you would be faced with the same difficulty — unless you were able to achieve total surprise, he would be able to transmute his outer skin into impenetrable titanium, and your machete would simply shatter. The same advisement applies to other forms of combat, such as trying to strike a vital nerve cluster to temporarily paralyze his legs or arms, or hitting him over the head with a blunt object in order to knock him unconscious. Either form of attack would require surprise, so that he would not have time to transmute his skin into titanium and ward off any and all blows.

"I am sincerely sorry I am unable to provide more helpful information," Super-Genius Jules said. "Suffice to say, I will continue to ponder this conundrum. Firstly, it is a fascinating puzzle. Secondly, I wish to prevent harm coming to you. Thirdly, I wish to prevent harm from coming to myself. If Hiro Matsuba discovers my existence, he would be honor-bound to slay me, as well, since I was once a part of Jules Duchon, and he has been paid to kill Jules Duchon. If your Jules is guilty of the crimes of body snatching and vivisection, then I am equally guilty, by extension."

"Oh, geeze," Maureen said. She felt completely deflated. She had been almost *certain* Super-Genius Jules would've had a solution for them. But she'd come up snake eyes. "If even a super-genius like you can't figure out a way to defeat Matter Master..."

"Do not despair yet, Maureen," Super-Genius Jules said, a hint of tenderness creeping into his otherwise robotic voice. "No problem is insolvable. As powerful and skillful as Hiro Matsuba is, he is not invincible. He must have a weakness which can be properly exploited. His only limitation, according to the anime film, is that he cannot utilize his matter-controlling powers on people and things beyond himself when he has transformed his epidermis into titanium armor, because then his special energy cannot penetrate his own skin to affect another. I will continue to ponder the problem. When I have determined a solution, I will contact you. Where are you and your Jules staying during this crisis? I assume you have temporarily abandoned your home."

"We're 'living,' if you can call it that, in Jules's Cadillac on the lowest level of the parking garage next to the Hotel Monteleone, the parking garage located on Iberville Street."

"I assumed as much. That is the only logical place for you to hide during the daylight hours, assuming you stay within the bounds of New Orleans. Might I strongly suggest that you both flee to the city the farthest away from New Orleans which you can reach during nighttime hours? The logical location would be Houston, a five hour drive away. Houston is four and a half times the size and extent of New Orleans. It offers the greatest number of potential hiding places for a pair of vampires of any city within reach."

"Jules — my Jules, I mean — won't leave New Orleans. He's gotten his vampiric powers back, and he won't leave Dr. Landrieu, his mother, and Emiko and Shogo behind. He thinks he can stop Matter Master somehow, before he kills us all."

"I see. How foolish of him; but not unexpected, given his extremely limited intellect and his emotional profile. At this time, fleeing is the only reasonable course of action, but your Jules is anything but reasonable. May I ask how he regained his vampiric powers? I regained mine through sheer mental concentration, a massive effort of brain power which is far beyond your Jules's abilities."

"Doodlebug hypnotized him into thinking he was the Hooded Terror back in the 1940s, and a Japanese spy named Tora, Tora, Tora had slipped him a drug which took away his vampiric powers. But Doodlebug also told him the drug would wear off."

"I see. So Rory relied upon the power of your Jules's belief in his own recovery to ensure that he would recover. Very clever of him."

"Jules," Maureen said, her face stricken with grief, "Doodlebug is dead."

"*Dead?*" Now Super-Genius Jules's face betrayed grief of its own, but only momentarily, before he brought his emotions fully under control. "Did you witness this happen?"

"No. But Jules spontaneously snapped out of his hypnosis, without Doodlebug being present to bring him out of it. Jules figures Matter Master must've gotten to him."

"That is a logical assumption. The hypnotic connection between Rory and your Jules would have been severed the moment Rory was transmuted into inert matter of some sort. I share your grief, Maureen. Rory was very dear to me, as well. I share all of your Jules's memories, you know. I remember turning Rory, an orphan, back in the darkest days of World War Two. I remember his exploits at my side as Doodlebug, the Wonder Boy. I remember his later turn to transvestism and the estrangement this caused between me and him. I fully recall his successful attempt to aid me during my conflict with Malice X, his patiently teaching me how to split into multiple forms. Without this skill, I, my present self, would never have come into being. So Rory, in an indirect way, is responsible for my own existence. I will mourn him as long as I remain incarnated upon Earth, Maureen."

A single tear rolled down Maureen's cheek. "Oh, Varney, I miss him already..." Maureen let the sentence trail off into silence.

"You have my full sympathy, Maureen. I will attempt to contact you once I have determined a way to defeat Hiro Matsuba. I would much prefer, however, to seek you out at the Hotel Monteleone parking garage and find that you have left for Houston. In such a case, should I determine how to kill or disable the Matter Master, I will take it upon myself to do so. My main advantage over him is that he is unaware of my existence, since the High Krewe, being ignorant of me, could not have informed him to be on the lookout for a super-intelligent twin of Jules Duchon.

"Be well, Maureen. I know your Jules has been listening to this conversation. I beg him to overcome his foolish sense of heroism and flee to Houston. He can take Amos and Mrs. Landrieu with the two of you, arranging for their coffins to be shipped to an apartment in Houston. Emiko and Shogo, having super-powers of their own, can take care of themselves. Please, I pray that you go to Houston, Maureen. I dearly desire for you to be safe."

Maureen felt a sudden surge of emotion. Her face nearly crumbled into tears, but she resisted the impulse. "Thank — thank you, Jules." She reached out and squeezed his hand, then kissed him on his cheek. She turned to walk back to her own Jules.

"Did you hear all that, Jules?" she asked him.

"Yeah, I heard," Jules said glumly.

"What do you think it means?"

"The smartest vampire in the world can't think of a solution, other than us running away to Houston, where Matter Master will eventually find us. What do I think it means? I think it means we're fucked."

* * * * *

Amos Landrieu absolutely hated the notion of leaving his wife Edna alone in their house. Rory had disappeared. That meant something bad had happened to him. Jules and Maureen were hiding in the basement parking lot next to the Monteleone Hotel, waiting for Super-Genius Jules to come up with a solution. So he and Edna were on their own. But they had run out of groceries, so he had driven to the nearest Sav-A-Center to grab a few emergency items. He had left Edna with a gun, a Beretta automatic. He carried an identical gun in his coat pocket. Its weight dragged his sport coat lower on the right side of his body.

He was half-way across the parking lot to his car when his cell phone rang. His heart jumped — was Edna in trouble or frightened and was calling him? He immediately dug his cell phone out of his other coat pocket.

"Hello? This is Amos. Is this Edna?"

"No, this is not Edna Landrieu," a voice unknown to Amos answered. The voice, he realized with a sinking feeling in the pit of his stomach, was tinged with a Japanese accent. *Matter Master*. "Edna Landrieu is unable to speak to you at the present time, Dr. Landrieu."

"What — what have you *done* to her?" he asked, dreading the answer.

"She was an exceedingly bad shot. The one bullet she aimed at me smashed a vase into tiny shards. But it appears she is far more proficient at knitting. Thus, to accede to her preferences, I turned her into a giant ball of yarn."

"You *didn't!* You — you *monster...*"

"If you wish for me to transform your wife back into her normal form, return to your home and allow me to immobilize you, Doctor. It is the only way I will agree to change your wife back into her original state."

"I'll be there, you goddamn son of a bitch."

Amos Landrieu pulled his vintage Mercedes into the narrow driveway next to his and Edna's home on Royal Street in the Bywater neighborhood, a district which had escaped the scourge of Hurricane Antonia's flooding.

He exited his car suffering from painful acid reflux. *I'm walking into my own death,* he said. *But surrendering to Matter Master is the only chance I have of saving Edna. Or is it? Edna may've been a terrible shot, but I'm not. I earned the rank of Marksman while serving as an Army doctor in Vietnam. Maybe Matter Master will be* expecting *me to meekly surrender. Maybe if I pull out my pistol as soon as I enter the door, I'll catch him by surprise?*

Amos steeled himself to do just that. As soon as he was next to his ruined front door (Matter Master had transformed it into paper, he saw, and simply pushed his way through it to enter the house and attack Edna), he pulled his Barretta out of his pocket. Then he leaped through the opening, spotted Matter Master standing in the corner, and got off two shots, one of which struck his foe squarely in the chest.

He heard a metallic ping. The bullet had bounced off.

"Very heroic, Dr. Landrieu," Matter Master said. "But having researched you and read of your service in your nation's Army, I assumed you might try something of the sort. Thus, I took proper precautions. Did you know I can apply my powers to my own self? I transmuted my outer skin into a set of armor made of titanium. It would take an armor-piercing anti-tank shell to penetrate this skin."

I'm a dead man, Amos thought. *All I can do now is bargain for Edna's life.* He saw the giant ball of yarn next to the couch in the living room, and his heart sank. "What do I need to do in order to get you to restore my wife to normal?"

"It's very simple, Dr. Landrieu. I will honor the terms of the bargain we struck on the phone. Toss aside your gun, walk over to me, and allow me to transform you into an inert form of matter. Then I will change your wife back to her original state. You have my word as a Japanese warrior who venerates the path of honor."

"Very well," Amos said. He threw the gun onto the floor. It skidded across the room until it hit the far wall. At that point, Matter Master's body began glowing with green energy. His titanium skin returned to human flesh.

"Here we go," Amos whispered to himself. "I hope there's a spot in heaven set aside for vampires who never drank human blood..."

He stepped within arm's length of Matter Master. The Japanese assassin reached out and touched him with his right hand. He again glowed with green energy, and sparks of that green energy leaped from his hand and fingertips into Amos Landrieu's body.

Amos felt himself beginning to transform. He knew not into what. Were he able to retain consciousness, he might have eventually realized that the Japanese assassin had transformed him into a six-foot-tall giant pill bottle, filled with giant tablets of aspirin.

Had Amos eyes to see with, he would have then watched Matter Master walk casually to the giant ball of yarn and touch it with his right hand. He would have seen green energy arc from that hand into the yarn. He would have seen his wife Edna emerge from her terrible transformation.

"Wha-whaaaaat?" she said. "What the heck did you do to me, you Jap fiend?" She then noticed the giant pill bottle and shrieked with surprise. "And what the heck is *that?*"

"That, my dear woman," Matter Master said, "is your husband, Dr. Amos Landrieu."

Edna began screaming. But she did not scream for long. Matter Master touched her a third time with his right hand and transformed her back into a giant ball of yarn.

Had Amos Landrieu still ears to hear with, he would have heard Hiro Matsuba say this: "Alas, my dear Dr. Landrieu, you were not precise enough in your bargain. As a warrior of honor, I fulfilled my part. I changed your wife back to her normal state. But you did not ask me to promise not to then change her again into a giant ball of yarn. Your loss, Doctor, but my gain. For I now have two more hostages with which to lure Maureen and Jules Duchon to me.

"I thank you, sir."

Had Amos Landrieu eyes to see with, he would have then seen Matter Master bow ironically to him. Had he a mouth to speak with, he would have screamed with frustration and rage.

Thirteen

EMIKO Tezuka opened the door to the room she shared with her cousin and co-*tarento* member of the Acme Talent Peerless Proficiencies Trio, Shogo Fukuda. Shogo, lying on one of the twin beds, looked up from watching television. It was just after ten P.M. Emiko noticed her cousin was watching some inane American animated comedy which focused on the astounding stupidity of an average American family. "<So?>" he said in Japanese. "<What pearls of wisdom did Super-Genius Jules share with you, cousin?>"

Emiko had known from the sour look on Super-Genius Jules's face as soon as he'd looked up from his card table and reading device that either he would not be cooperative or he would have no solution to share with her. It ended up being the latter.

"<There is no need for you to be so sarcastic, Shogo,>" Emiko said. "<It is true that he did not have any fresh ideas to share with me that would help us deal with the Matter Master. However, he *did* give a qualified thumbs-up to *my* plan.>"

"<And what is a 'qualified thumbs-up,' cousin?>"

"<He said my plan of stranding the Matter Master as a two-dimensional anime version of himself so that he could not utilize his powers has an approximately thirty percent chance of succeeding. This is because I must touch him. Super-Genius Jules said he did not have the data to calculate whether the Matter Master would be able to touch and

transform me while I am in my anime form — thus, the uncertainty of success.>"

"<And what of *my* plan, cousin?>"

"<*Your* plan, Shogo?>" she said disdainfully. "<You mean turning into Cutie-Scary Man and whacking him on the head with a large club? Given that the Matter Master can transmute his outer skin into a suit of nearly indestructible titanium armor, Super-Genius Jules gave *that* plan an approximately four percent chance of success.>"

Shogo frowned. "<Well, what does he know, anyway? He's just a goofball with a weird, tall forehead.>" He jumped off the bed, went to the closet, and retrieved the special padded box which held the last two of his energy-charged *otakus.* "<Let's go. I'll let you try your way first, and then if that doesn't work, I'll give it my best shot. I still think I can jump him before he has a chance to transform his skin or to touch me with his right hand. All it takes is a bit of sneaking up on him, and then one good '*whack!*' on the head...>"

Emiko motioned for her cousin to sit back down. "<Put those last two shrunken fan-boys away, Shogo. We aren't going anywhere tonight.>"

"<Why not? We are both well rested. Let's go! Why give Matter Master another night in which to strike?>"

"<Because either of our plans demand *stealth,* Shogo! Think this through. All the inhabitants of the High Krewe's compound are *vampires.* The persons the Matter Master is hunting are *vampires.* When do vampires sleep?"

"<In the daytime, of course.>"

"<So if we don't want to be seen by any of the members of the High Krewe, we must invade their compound in the *daytime.* Also, thus far, the Matter Master has been mainly active at night. I suspect that, for the duration of this assignment, he, too, sleeps during the daytime, since he prefers to hunt his quarry at night, when they are active and away from

their hidden coffins.>"

Emiko saw understanding dawn on her cousin's face. "<Ohhh... I get it now. Okay, I will go back to watching *Adult Swim.* Those American cartoons crack me up!>"

Emiko and Shogo waited until an hour past dawn, in order to (they hoped) give Matter Master a chance to go to sleep. Then they took a cab to the boundary of Orleans Parish and Jefferson Parish, which was the bridge from the east bank to the west bank of the Seventeenth Street Canal. Emiko paid the cab driver. Only after the cab had turned around and headed back towards downtown did Emiko begin leading her cousin, who was carrying the box containing their last two *otakus,* through the woods which separated Metairie Road from the High Krewe's walled compound.

Shogo scowled as he pushed thorny brambles away from his face. The sunlight was not yet strong, and the going was thick. "<Wouldn't it be easier to simply walk up their long driveway? It is the daytime. They are all asleep.>"

Emiko stopped walking. She turned to her cousin. "<Shogo, are you not aware there are security cameras mounted on top of the outer wall of their compound?>"

Shogo rolled his eyes towards the sky. "<Of *course* I am aware of that, Emiko. But it is the daytime, so there is no one who is watching the security monitors. They are all asleep!>"

"<But what if when the cameras detect movement, they automatically set off an alarm to awaken the vampires? If the windows are blocked with heavy curtains or shutters to keep out the sunlight, as I suspect they are, the vampires can emerge from their coffins during daylight hours without fear of being dissolved. Then they will be free to attempt to attack me, or to rouse the Matter Master. Or what if the Matter Master himself is awake and is watching the security monitors? No, Shogo, even

though it is the daytime, *still* must we be stealthy.>"

She began walking again, pushing the low-lying brambles out of her way. When they were about a third of the way through the woods, or a hundred yards distant from the compound's outer security wall, Emiko paused again. "<Shogo, give me one of the energy-charged fan-boys. I want to make my change into my anime form here, where the green flash of my transformation will be blocked by the trees and thus not picked up by any of the security cameras.>"

Shogo complied. He opened up the padded carrying case, then removed one of the tiny coffin-like inner boxes. Green light shone through the air holes of the box. He opened it and removed the comatose *otaku,* then handed it to his cousin.

"<Remember to catch him, Shogo, as soon as I transform. I will be unable to hold him then, and he might be badly injured should he fall to the ground.>"

Shogo again rolled his eyes heavenward. "<Do not worry, cousin, I will be careful. No harm will come to him.>"

A songbird emitted its lovely cry. The forest smelled of fresh pine cones, Emiko noticed. *Such a beautiful forest to surround such a sinister house,* she thought.

Beneath the shelter of the pine trees and oak trees, she firmly grasped the greenly glowing *otaku's* tiny waist in both her hands and held him over her head. Then she closed her eyes so she could concentrate. She focused her thoughts on images of herself as a two-dimensional image of Anime Girl, star attraction of the Acme Talent Peerless Proficiencies Trio, and on thoughts of green energy flowing from the *otaku* down through her fingers and into her arms and body, empowering her.

Three seconds later, she became a two-dimensional version of herself, stretched out along the forest floor. Looking up, she saw the *otaku,* no longer held in her hands, begin to fall, but was enormously relieved to see Shogo catch him.

"<Okay, Shogo,>" she said from the ground. "<Here is the deal. I am your older cousin, so you *must* do as I say. No rushing in prematurely. Only if I fail to re-emerge from that compound within thirty minutes should you attempt to rescue me. I will spend that time searching the house for the Matter Master. Pray that I find him sleeping peacefully in his bed.>"

With that said, she flowed along the forest floor until she reached the clearing surrounding the security wall. She waited until no rotating security cameras were pointed at her section of the clearing, then flowed speedily across this open space. She flowed up the surface of the wall until she reached the first of the cameras. Then she flowed directly into its lens.

Her abrupt entry as a being made of energy caused the camera to short out. She raced the short along the buried wires of the network until she reached one of the monitors connected to the camera. Then, having won her race, she emerged from the monitor into the main compound of the High Krewe. Instantly after she emerged, the monitor's screen, distorted by the short, exploded behind her. Had she been in her three-dimensional form, her back would have been peppered by sharp glass.

She heard alarm Klaxons going off. The malfunction in the camera, the resulting short, or the exploding monitor must've triggered an automatic alarm. She would have to work fast, before all the inhabitants of the house were aroused from sleep. She prayed that the Matter Master was a sound sleeper, and that the doors of the bedrooms, in addition to the lids of the vampires' coffins, were thick enough to keep the alarm's noise from the ears of the vampires.

She flowed from room to room, searching desperately for the Matter Master. But she failed to find him. She entered the library, the kitchen, the den, the living room, the dining hall, and a dozen bedrooms which contained luxurious rosewood coffins. But no Matter Master.

She received a most unpleasant surprise when she entered the last of the bedrooms, the most opulent one she had yet seen. Its vampire occupant had emerged from his coffin. She rushed him, not wanting to give him a chance to escape the room and awaken the Matter Master. She would transform him into an anime facsimile of himself and trap him in the two-dimensional world she inhabited—

But then he did something completely unexpected. He transformed into *mist*. She rushed into the mist, and suddenly she was falling through a seemingly infinite dimension of complete darkness and absolute cold, with no surfaces for her to cling to or flow upon. Then she emerged into another completely dark space, but this one had surfaces. Rather than being infinite in expanse, this one was terribly confining. She barely had space to flow. She estimated her available space was about seven feet by three feet by two feet, or less than fifty square feet.

"Let me out of here!" she screamed in frustrated fury.

Then she heard the vampire's voice from outside this elongated box she was trapped within. "Let you out?" he said. "But you have just been introduced to my coffin, dear. It is quite air-tight, which means no light can escape. That also means *you* cannot escape, does it not? Am I correct in assuming you are Anime Girl, one of the allies of Jules Duchon with whom he became friendly after the recent Hurricane Antonia disaster? Your countryman Hiro Matsuba, knowing how quickly rumors travel through the Japanese underworld, warned me that the members of the Acme Talent Peerless Proficiencies Trio might have heard of his assignment and could potentially travel to New Orleans to assist Duchon with a defense against him. By the way, do not attempt to transform back into your three-dimensional form and force the coffin lid open. I have already summoned one of the servants with a hammer and long nails. Oh, in fact, here he is now. Otranto, please do me the honor of nailing my coffin shut."

Emiko heard the terrible, sharp sounds of nails being hammered into wood all around her.

"And here comes your countryman," the main vampire said. "Good morning, Mr. Matsuba. I am sorry that you have been awakened from your rest by the alarm. Thank you for alerting me that Anime Girl, if she sought entrance to the compound, would travel through the security camera system, and that her entry would set off the alarm. Thus, I was prepared for her when she found me. As we had planned, I trapped her in my coffin."

"You are very welcome, Besthoff-*san,*" a Japanese accented voice which Emiko assumed belonged to Hiro Matsuba said. "And thank you for so efficiently trapping her. She was the one member of the Acme Talent Peerless Proficiencies Trio who had the best chance of defeating me. The other two are almost beneath my contempt. By the way, where will you sleep now that Anime Girl occupies your coffin?"

"Oh, don't worry about that, Mr. Matsuba. I have several spare coffins I can use in its place. What you need to be concerned about now is whether or not Anime Girl's two partners will attempt to storm the compound and rescue her."

"I will take care of it," the Matter Master said, "with enormous pleasure."

Shogo checked his watch. It was 9:07 A.M. Exactly a half-hour since Emiko had entered the security camera, and the five cameras atop the wall had shorted out one by one.

She's in trouble, he thought. *Ready or not, High Krewe, here I come...*

He removed his very last energy-packed *otaku* from his padded case and box. He noticed this *otaku* had been transformed by Emiko back in Hiroshima into a minuscule Hello, Kitty. That was fine. Shogo's becoming a savage jungle cat was certainly appropriate, given the dire situation.

Just as Emiko had a half-hour before, Shogo held the glowing *otaku* above his head with both hands. He closed his eyes to concentrate. He focused on drawing energy from the *otaku* and becoming a man-sized Hello, Kitty.

Seconds later, he felt the tingly green energy, which had originated months ago in Hiroshima at the opening of a shopping mall when Kenji, the Bonsai Master, had first shrunk the *otaku* down to his current tiny size. The energy raced from the *otaku* through Kenji's hands, down his arms, and throughout his body. Kenji sensed his own shape changing to match that of the *otaku,* although far larger.

He placed the *otaku,* still glowing green but more faintly, back in his box and placed the box into the carrying case which also held a box with the other weakly glowing *otaku* inside. Once he and Emiko were done with the need for their super-powers (he prayed his cousin was yet unharmed), he would restore the two *otakus* to their original forms and size, minus about twenty to thirty pounds apiece. He had already restored the other two *otaku* which Emiko had used since their arrival in New Orleans; those particular fan-boys they had already sent home to Japan.

Now, having set the *otaku* aside (he hid the carrying case in a nook between the low-lying branches of a tree), Shogo was free to undergo the second stage of his transformation, which was also powered with the energy he had borrowed from the *otaku.* He pressed his palms together, closed his eyes, and concentrated on assuming the Scary version of his Cutie-Scary Man identity. He imagined himself with claws the length of Arabian daggers. He imagined himself with glowing red eyes in place of Hello, Kitty's kindly black eyes. He imagined himself with black fur, rather than pink fur, and fur so stiff it could act as body armor.

He had done this sort of thing many dozens of times before. The secondary transformation came over him effortlessly, as simple and easy as changing clothes.

Now that he was Scary Kitty, it was time to seriously shake things up for the High Krewe and their hired flunky, the Matter Master. If any of them had harmed so much as a fingernail of his cousin's, he would make terrible use of his dagger-length claws. They were sharp enough, when driven by his prodigious strength, to shred iron.

He stalked silently on two legs through the remainder of the woods to the outer wall of the High Krewe's compound. The five security cameras still sputtered and smoked from the damage Emiko had done to them thirty minutes before, so Shogo did not worry about being detected. He used his claws to climb the wall and then leaped down the other side, landing on a swath of carefully tended grass.

"<What a fabulous mansion and estate,>" he whispered to himself as he entered the compound. He loped into a central courtyard which contained a formal garden filled with roses of all different colors, at the center of which burbled an impressive fountain with a statue of a large bat mounted on a stone obelisk; water flowed from the bat's mouth into the surrounding pool below.

"<I think I will enter the main house through its back door,>" he whispered to himself. "<That way, I may still preserve the element of surprise.>"

Yet Shogo himself was the one to be rudely surprised. The Matter Master stepped out from the shadows of one of the subsidiary buildings. "<Ah, Cutie-Scary Man,>" he said. "<Your cousin Anime Girl has already been dealt with—>"

"<Have you hurt her, foul assassin?>" Shogo cried across the courtyard. His enemy stood on the opposite side of the fountain, still shaded by the shadows cast by the surrounding buildings.

"<Oh, I did nothing to her. She is yet unharmed, unlike some of your other friends. Where is the third member of your trio, the Bonsai Master? He is the member of the Acme Talent Peerless Proficiencies Trio whom I look forward to dueling with the most. You, Cutie-Scary Man, are unfortunately almost beneath my notice.>"

The Matter Master stepped out into the sunlight. Shogo saw that his silver skin glinted brightly in the sun. "<What—?>" Shogo said.

"<I see you are surprised, my feline friend. Anticipating combat with you and the Bonsai Master, who can capture energy from any nearby

object and hurl that energy as destructive force, I took the precaution of transforming my skin into titanium armor.>"

"<My claws are sharp enough to shred iron, villain!>"

"<Ah, but not titanium, sadly for you. You are over-matched, Cutie-Scary Man. Call for your confederate, the Bonsai Master. At least he will give me a fight worth remembering.>"

"<He is hiding in another part of the compound,>" Shogo lied. Even though Kenji was, in truth, thousands of miles away, still, it made sense to keep the Matter Master off-balance. "<He will join the fight if and when I fail to subdue you.>"

The Matter Master strode toward him. "<Then let us begin without delay, you ridiculous creature.>"

"<If I die today, then let it be with the honor appropriate to a Japanese warrior,>" Shogo said with the greatest conviction. Then he rushed at Matter Master.

He raked him with his claws. Just as Matter Master had claimed, Shogo's fearsome claws failed to even scratch his titanium skin. Instead, Shogo's claws bent backward. One broke entirely off, and Shogo howled with pain.

Matter Master gave Shogo a savage karate chop at the base of his neck. The titanium fist landed with the force of a battering ram. Shogo fell over backward, an ugly bruise forming beneath his fur. He again leaped toward Matter Master. This time, he did not bother trying to rake him with his claws. Instead, he grabbed both of Matter Master's shoulders, lifted him high above his feline head, and hurled his foe into the fountain.

Matter Master smashed into the stone obelisk holding the statue of a bat. The surface of the stone obelisk cracked upon impact. But Shogo could see that Matter Master, protected by his titanium armor, was unhurt by the mighty blow.

Shina Myoushu was by far the most formidable foe he had ever faced. Fighting him made Shogo's battle against Jules Duchon, when Duchon had been a savage giant rabbit, seem like a child's game of tag.

Matter Master picked himself up from the pool and stepped out of the water. "<Were you hoping I would rust?>" he said. "<If so, I must disappoint you. Titanium does not rust. Now, let us bring this farce to an end. Trade blows with me, if you dare.>"

Shogo dared. He simply could not pass up the challenge. He stood toe to toe with Matter Master, using his superior agility (Matter Master was slowed by the weight of his massive armor) to dodge most of Matter Master's blows.

But his own blows did nothing more than badly bruise his knuckles. And Matter Master managed to land enough karate chops that Shogo felt his innermost organs were being pulverized. The *clang!* of Shogo's blows began to be followed more and more frequently by the sickening *thud!* of Matter Master's steely blows against Shogo's vulnerable fur and flesh.

At last, battered and exhausted, Shogo sagged to the ground. His vision swirled like the eye of a typhoon. "<Ah, you are nearly ready,>" he heard Matter Master say above him. Then he felt a titanium fist grasp the loose scruff of his neck and drag him toward the damaged fountain.

Matter Master lifted him up by his neck. Then he plunged his face into the water, again and again.

Shogo sputtered and coughed. His lungs began to fill with water. Matter Master lifted him once more. This time, he dropped him to the ground. Shogo coughed helplessly and furiously. Aside from coughing, he could not manage to move.

He saw a flash of green light above him. When his vision cleared somewhat, he thought he saw that Matter Master had changed his skin back into human flesh.

He saw his enemy reaching for him with his right hand. That hand pressed against his chest. The green flash of energy arcing from Matter Master's hand into his body was the last thing Shogo saw before his eyes turned to buttons and darkness overtook him.

Had he still possessed functioning eyes, Shogo would have been stunned to see himself transformed into a man-sized plush doll of Hello, Kitty, replete with pink polyester fur.

Fourteen

DAYTIME in the French Quarter. It was only a few months since the devastation of Hurricane Antonia, which had flooded nearly all of New Orleans outside the French Quarter, parts of Uptown, and Algiers on the West Bank of the Mississippi. But even so, the tourists, learning that the Vieux Carré had been essentially unaffected by the storm, flocked back to the city and its world-famous French Quarter in droves.

Walking the streets of the Quarter, they became hungry. Some weren't in the mood for a regular meal; others couldn't afford many regular meals in the Quarter's oftentimes pricey establishments. So they entered the gift shops and tee-shirt shops and small grocery stores and convenience stores, searching for snacks.

One cheap snack they often chanced upon was the Bunny Bread Banana Snack Cake. They ate the little locally baked cakes with abandon, savoring its delicious banana flavor. If a few of them bothered to pay close attention to that flavor, though, they might notice it seemed just a touch *off*, that the sweetness was marred by a tiny metallic aftertaste.

The source of that aftertaste, which was actually the taste of iron in blood? It was minute traces of the blood of Emiko Tezuka and Shogo Fukuda.

During his recent visit to New Orleans, Shogo had so enjoyed battling Jules Duchon when the vampire had been transformed by drinking

Emiko's and Shogo's blood into a vicious six-foot-tall rabbit, he had attempted to ensure that his delightful contest of strength would be repeated. He saw that many of the French Quarter's gift shops and convenience stores sold bunches of Bunny Bread Banana Snack Cakes to tourists; Jules's own mother sold them in Jules's tour shop, even. So Shogo had snuck into the Bunny Bread factory at night and secretly adulterated the tremendous mixing tub of Banana Snack Cake batter with sizable quantities of his and Emiko's blood. He figured the tourists would then arrive at Jules's *Real* Vampires of New Orleans tour with traces of the Japanese super-heroes' blood already in their veins, and when they donated blood to Jules and his vampire friends in exchange for admission to the tour, those traces of Emiko's and Shogo's blood would be eventually ingested by Jules, turning him into a marvelous, fighting-mad monster again.

But in this instance, the vampire who would be affected wouldn't be Jules Duchon...

* * * * *

The night after Jules and Maureen had their meeting in Jackson Square with Super-Genius Jules, they sat for hours in the front seats of Jules's Cadillac in the basement parking garage next to the Monteleone Hotel, the key in the ignition, listening to the radio while waiting for a solution to their predicament from their genius friend, for want of anything better to do.

"Jules," Maureen said, her mouth filled with a big bite of a Ding-Dong snack cake, "I'm sick and tired of listening to Sports Talk with Buddy D. Can't we listen to something *else?* I'm bored to death of hearing callers phoning in with all their bitching about the Saints' wide receivers and linebacker corps. I wanna listen to some contemporary hits, okay?"

"But Maureen," Jules whined, "the coach is gonna be interviewed in the next segment. He's gonna announce some mid-season personnel changes that are gonna salvage the season. I wanna hear that. Can't you wait just another half-hour or so?"

"Jules, I think if I listen to another half-hour of Sports Talk, I will go *insane.*"

"Aren't you distractin' yourself with stuffin' your face with them Ding-Dongs, anyway? What's the difference?"

Maureen scowled. "Oh, Jules, did you have to *mention* that? Now I feel *guilty.* But you know what I'm up to? It's *stress-eating.* I think I'll fall apart with anxiety unless I keep it up. And in the meantime, I'm adding who-knows-how-many inches to my waistline and hips." She thought for a minute. "Hey, you know what? At least I could be eating something healthier for me than Ding-Dongs! Bunny Bread Banana Snack Cakes have real *bananas* in them, so I'd be getting some potassium, at least. You know that big stash of Bunny Bread Banana Cakes we've got at the house to sell to the tourists? They haven't been selling, so we've still got half a carton left. How about I walk over to the house real quick and get them, and you can sit here and listen to your Sports Talk?"

Now it was Jules's turn to scowl. "How about we *both* walk over to the house and get them *after* the coach's interview? I'm not lettin' you outta this parking garage without me, hon. Or better yet, why don't we hit one of the convenience stores outside the Quarter after the coach's interview and buy your Banana Snack Cakes there? There's always a chance Matter Master has staked out our house."

"Jules, don't be *ridiculous.* Matter Master probably thinks we're hiding somewhere in Houston or Lake Charles by now. He's probably already gone to those cities to search for us. He won't be staking out our house. Later, we can ask Emiko to spy on the High Krewe for us through their smart phones or computers and tell us exactly where Matter Master is. In the meantime, though, we'd better save up our money, because we've got no idea *how long* we're going to be in hiding. You've got to spend money on gas, and I've got to spend money on food, because that little stash of tourists' blood in our refrigerator isn't going to last very long. And I want to save it all for you, since the only thing you can eat besides blood is dog chow when you turn into a wolf. And I don't think you want to go back to living on dog chow."

"You got that right."

"So let me save us some money and go back to our house so I can fetch the Bunny Bread Banana Cakes we've already paid for, okay?"

Jules sighed, turned off the radio, and turned the key in the ignition to the Off position. "I told you, I ain't gonna let you go wandering around the Quarter on your own. I'll go with you."

Jules and Maureen reached their house without incident. Jules insisted that they wait in the shadows down the block from their house for a half-hour before entering, to see if they spotted Matter Master lurking about. The villain did not show his face.

Once they were inside, Maureen was delighted to see the variety of snacks and junk food they had stashed in the closet in their living room to sell to the tourists taking Jules's vampire tours. "Just *look* at all this stuff!" she said. "Holy Varney, I could blow up to three hundred pounds if I took all this crap back to the car with us. But I think I'll just take the Bunny Bread Snack Cakes and that carton of Wondrous Woman Bubble Gum."

"What do you want the bubble gum for?" Jules said. "You've never chewed gum before."

"I don't want it for the *gum,* Jules. I'll throw away the gum. It's the little mini-comics I want to look at, the mini-comics that are printed on trading cards inside of the gum packages. Didn't I just act out the role of Wondrous Woman for a couple of nights? I never used to read her comics back in World War Two, and I haven't read them since the war, either. But now I'm curious. If I can read some little stories about her and her villains, it'll help me pass the time while sitting in the Cadillac. Especially if you let me listen to contemporary hits while I'm reading. And while I'm reading, I'll have to eat my snacks more slowly, between opening up the bubble gum packs and digging out the trading cards. That way, maybe I won't put on so much weight with this stress-eating of mine."

"Well, okay," Jules said. "I guess I owe you a treat after makin' you listen to so many hours of Sports Talk. Take whatever you want, hon. I'll carry it all back to the car for you. In the meantime, I'll grab me a couple of pints of blood out of the refrigerator."

Once safely ensconced in the car again, Jules drank his blood. Maureen ate like a demoness and read the Wondrous Woman mini-comics almost as voraciously. "Jules, these little comics are a *hoot!*" she said with a mouth stuffed full of banana cake. "I just *love* them! And the villain, this musclebound gal called Slamazon, she's an even *better* character than Wondrous Woman. She spends all her time pulling evil pranks on men, like sticking bombs in urinals that explode whenever guys take a whiz. Isn't that *great?* This is some pretty hilarious stuff! It's like the writers of these little mini-comics are doing for Wondrous Woman what the TV producers did for Batman with that show from the sixties, the one with Adam West. They've actually managed to make the character a laugh riot!"

"Glad you're havin' yourself a good time, hon," Jules said glumly. Maureen had picked out a radio station that played the biggest hits of the eighties. So Jules, a lover of classic jazz and blues, had been stuck listening for the past hour to the likes of Depeche Mode, the Pet Shop Boys, and Adam Ant.

Forty-five minutes later, after she'd emptied all but one pack from the carton of Bunny Bread Banana Snack Cakes, Jules saw Maureen clutch her stomach. She moaned. "Oh, Jules, I think I might've overdone it on the snack cakes..."

Jules looked at her face with alarm. "Yeah, you sure *did,* hon —

you're turning green!"

In fact, Maureen was *glowing* green. The only time Jules had ever seen Maureen glow green like that had been three months ago, when they'd both been bingeing on Emiko's donated blood to see what it would do (Kenji's blood had gotten them both high). Then, Jules had turned into a six-foot-tall white rabbit and Maureen had enlarged to six hundred pounds. Was she about to turn enormously fat again?

He lifted his hand to cover his eyes from the anticipated flash of green light, but he wasn't fast enough, so he ended up getting dazzled, anyway. Blindly, he groped for Maureen, wondering (with delicious anticipation) if he would feel armfuls of soft blubber again. "Are you all right, hon?" he asked with his eyes closed. Instead, his hand grasped a very muscular upper arm.

"Get your hand off me, you inferior *male!*"

An *extremely* powerful grip displaced his hand. The voice had come from Maureen. But it was as low as a man's voice... whatever Maureen had turned into this time, it wasn't a sexually alluring, submissive fatty like before.

His vision cleared. He could see what Maureen had changed into now. She was over six feet tall (the top of her head touched the Cadillac's roof liner), with long, wavy black hair, a Grecian nose, and very well-defined musculature, like a lady body builder. Also, she wore a pair of immense metal bracelets, one on each wrist; they covered most of her forearms. Jules saw that part of the plastic and metal of the seat Maureen was sitting on had disappeared — that, he assumed, was where the extra mass had come from. "Uh, Wondrous Woman...?" he asked uncertainly.

"How *dare* you call me that, you male piece of dog excrement!" Maureen said. "I am Wondrous Woman's arch-foe, *Slamazon!*"

"Ohh, boy..." Jules muttered. "Look, uh, Slamazon, you ain't plannin' on doin' nothin' *crazy,* are you? Like pullin' pranks on guys by explodin' urinals and stuff?"

"I have no time for such trivialities!" Slamazon announced. "I shall indeed indulge in some mayhem, but it shall only be for the purpose of attracting Matter Master!"

"Oh, no, Maureen, you *can't* mean that— "

"Of *course* I can! And call me Slamazon, for that is who I am! I shall beat Matter Master to a bloody pulp, then sing my Amazon victory song over his rotting male corpse! I am assured of being victorious, for the High Krewe made the mistake of summoning a member of the *weaker sex* to act as their assassin!"

"I ain't lettin' you outta this car, Maureen," Jules said. He pressed the button that locked all the doors in the car, and then pressed a second button which disabled all lock buttons but his.

Slamazon laughed. "*Ha!* You ape-brained male! Do you truly think locking me in will stop me?" With one mighty shove, she dislodged the passenger-side door from its hinges and sent it skidding across the otherwise empty parking garage.

"Holy Mother of Jesus!" Jules exclaimed. "You're as strong as the *real* Slamazon!" His tongue burned like he'd just bit down on a jalapeno pepper, having desecrated the names of both Mother Mary and Jesus Christ, but he couldn't be concerned with the smoke pouring out of his mouth right now. "Maureen! Slamazon! Come *back!* No matter how strong you are, Matter Master will make an omelet outta you!"

But Slamazon's super-powerful legs had already propelled her up the parking lot's ramp and out the exit.

Jules hustled over to Super-Genius Jules's tarot card table in Jackson Square as fast as his fat legs would allow. "Super-Genius Jules!" he said, wheezing and breathing hard. "You and me, we got us a *load* of trouble!"

Super-Genius Jules calmly looked up from his reading device; clearly, he was not at all alarmed that Jules was alarmed. "Are you referring to the matter of Matter Master? Surely you remember that Maureen informed me of that whole predicament and all its ramifications. Rest assured, my inferior twin, my massive brain is hard at work on a solution— "

Jules shook his head wildly. "No! No! It's not Matter Master this time! It's *Maureen!*"

Now Super-Jules's eyes narrowed. He placed the reading device down on his card table. "What about Maureen, Jules?"

"She's turned into Slamazon, Wondrous Woman's arch-enemy!"

"Wondrous Woman and Slamazon are comic book characters, created by writer Harold N. Mitchner and artist J. 'Lemon' Stravinsky in 1940— "

"I *know* that, you genius-dummy, you! It's gotta be Emiko's and Shogo's blood all over again! That's the only explanation!"

"What are you talking about, Jules? Did Emiko and Shogo donate more blood to you? If they did, would either you or Maureen actually be so foolish as to drink it, knowing what it did to you three months ago?"

"Look, I *know* this sounds crazy, but their blood must've somehow gotten mixed in with the batter for Bunny Bread Banana Snack Cakes. Maureen's been chowin' down on those things all night. That's all she's eaten or drank tonight, I swear! And she's been readin' little mini-comics about Wondrous Woman and Slamazon, so Slamazon was fresh on her mind when she transformed."

Super-Genius Jules paused a second to think. "It certainly sounds like the effects of Emiko's blood," he said. "This makes more sense than it seems. I recall, from my time spent as a part of you, before my creation, that Shogo dearly loved battling you when his and his cousin Emiko's blood turned you into an evil giant rabbit. His self-esteem swelled like never before when the crowds in the French Quarter, who watched him thoroughly pummel you, cheered him as a hero. I postulate that he suffers from an inferiority complex of long standing, due to his knowledge that his super-hero forerunners in Japan, those who were active in the 1960s and 1970s, had many opportunities to battle monsters and super-criminals, but Shogo had come too late on the scene and was thus relegated to cutting ribbons at shopping center openings and performing for charitable events, like a clown or trained monkey.

"It is very possible that, before he left New Orleans for Japan, he infiltrated the Bunny Bread factory and emptied bags of his and Emiko's blood into the batter for the Banana Snack Cakes, knowing they are popular with tourists in the French Quarter and that you yourself sold them at your mother's ticket collection table in your living room. He assumed, and rightfully so, that drinking the blood of tourists who had consumed Bunny Bread Banana Snack Cakes would eventually result in your return to an evil, monstrous form which he could battle. Only his timing and aim were off, because Maureen suffered the effects from directly consuming the snack cakes herself."

"Excellent summary, Einstein," Jules said. "Now that we know what caused it, what are we gonna *do* about it? I came to you because I'd come up with a formula to counteract the effects of Shogo's blood three months ago, during those few hours right before you split off from me when *I* was Super-Genius Jules. But an hour after you'd split off from me, right after I'd had a chance in Doc Landrieu's lab to mix up one batch, the formula vanished from my normal-sized brain— "

"*Sub*-normal sized brain," Super-Genius Jules interjected.

"Whatever — this is no time for jokes, especially not at my expense. Can't you see I'm stressed to the max? Don't you love Maureen as much as I do? You know what she's up to right now? She's super-strong, and she's bound and determined to cause a big ruckus to attract Matter Master— "

"Wait — she *wants* Matter Master to come to her?"

"*Yeah!* That's what I'm telling you, you idjit! She's become super-evil Slamazon, the *man-hater!* She wants to bash Matter Master's face in 'cause the High Krewe *dared* to send an example of 'the weaker sex' after her to assassinate her! Slamazon's pride ain't gonna allow for that! But he's gonna make *mincemeat* outta her, Super-Genius!"

Super-Genius Jules rubbed his chin thoughtfully. "We must get to Amos Landrieu's lab so that I can create another batch of my formula to counteract Shogo's blood. After we have somehow gotten her to ingest it, she will stay Slamazon for the next three nights, just as your mother stayed a human vacuum cleaner for three nights before changing back to herself. But at least she will no longer have evil tendencies, thanks to my formula counteracting Shogo's blood. She will be rational. She will be willing to listen to reason and avoid the Matter Master until I can think of a plan to defeat him. You say she is super-strong and hates all members of the male sex?"

"Yeah."

"Then we'd better create an aerosol spray version of my formula. That shouldn't be difficult, not with the equipment in Amos Landrieu's lab. Can you drive us there?"

"Well, my car's kinda banged up," Jules said, "but it's drivable. You can ride with me, so long as you don't mind holdin' onto the dashboard so's you don't fly outta the car when I make a left turn."

Jules pulled into his mother's and step-father's driveway. He saw the broken front window, actually a glass French door. "Uh, oh," he said. "That don't look good..."

The two of them got out of the car (Super-Genius Jules just slid out, not having a door to open) and climbed the steps to the darkened house's front porch. "Don't look like nobody's home," Jules said. "But I guess hope springs eternal..." He rang the bell. No one came to the door. Jules called through the broken French door: "Mom? Amos?"

There was no answer. *Oh, shit,* Jules thought. *Matter Master's already gotten to them. Don't panic don't panic don't panic...* "We better go inside," he said.

They stepped through the broken door. Several chairs had been overturned. Jules saw holes in the wall — bullet holes? Hadn't Amos said he was going to buy guns for him and for Edna?

"This don't look good," Jules said. "This don't look good at all..."

"I worry for your mother and step-father, too, Jules," Super-Genius Jules said. "But right now, our greatest concern is for Maureen's safety."

"You don't gotta remind *me* of that, pal," Jules said with a warning tone in his voice. "She's *my wife,* the love of my life. Shit, I love her so much, I'm rhymin'. C'mon. Let's head down the stairs to the lab."

Jules turned on the lights in the basement lab. Once he'd descended five of the ten steps, however, he saw there was no sense in continuing to walk down. The lab had been pulverized. The floor was covered with broken glass, spilled chemicals, and shattered scientific equipment.

"Whoever did this," Super-Genius Jules said, "had a burning desire to punish Amos Landrieu..."

"Matter Master. It had to be Matter Master. Couldn't be anybody else."

They climbed back up to the disheveled living room. Nervous, looking for something to do with his hands, Jules worked on digging a bullet out of the wall. "I have bad news to share," Super-Genius Jules said to him. "I can still create the counteraction formula, but even my super-brain can think of no way to rent a lab facility this late at night. Taco Bell take out I can locate at this hour; lab facilities, no. Oh, that was a joke to ease tension, in case you misunderstood my intent. You see, the earliest I could create the formula for us would be tomorrow evening. But I estimate there is a 98.9 percent chance that the Matter Master will locate Maureen tonight, given that she is making no attempt to hide herself, and is in fact attempting to attract his attention."

"Well, the one saving grace is that she don't look a thing like herself anymore..."

"That won't matter," Super-Genius Jules said. "Matter Master, being a meta-human super-hero himself, will be fully aware that a female meta-human named 'Slamazon' did not exist until tonight outside of the comic books. He will assume it is Maureen in disguise, and that her feats of super-strength are due to her vampiric nature. He does not realize that she lacks all of the typical vampiric super-abilities, except for when she has been transformed by Emiko's blood, then turned evil by Shogo's."

"Let's turn on the TV over there and see if we can locate Maureen. The late local news is about to come on."

Jules switched on Amos's and Edna's ancient console TV. The newscaster, John McBundy, had an astonished look on his face. "Ladies and gentlemen," he said to the camera, "the live footage you are about to see beggars belief... It appears New Orleans has been invaded by a genuine super-being calling herself 'Slamazon'..."

Jules watched with a sinking feeling in his stomach. "Oh, good Lord," he said (feeling his tongue beginning to blister again). "She's attacking the main Police Headquarters. She's surrounded by half the NOPD, it looks like, but she's tossin' them around like bowlin' pins and tippin' over their squad cars..." Then he saw something which truly beggared belief. One of the officers aimed his service pistol at her and fired. Slamazon/Maureen blocked the bullet with one of her steel bracelets covering her forearms. "Holy Mackerel! Did you see that? Did you? She just blocked a bullet, just like a *real* Amazon from the comics!"

"It is incredible that Emiko's blood could grant such abilities," Super-Genius Jules said. "However, given that she is able to turn her *otaku* fans cute, or *kawaii,* and then transform herself into a two-dimensional anime form, perhaps I should not be so astounded by what ingesting her blood has done to Maureen."

"I've got to get over there," Jules said.

"What do you plan to do? She will not listen to you. Yes, you are her husband. But you are also a member of the despised male sex. Seeing you, remembering, perhaps, that she 'degraded' herself by marrying you— " Super-Genius Jules hid a quick smile with his hand; "—she will likely kill you out of her sense of humiliation at ever having been connected with you in an intimate fashion."

Jules headed for the broken French door and his damaged car. "You don't think I *know* that? But I've got a plan!"

"What *sort* of a plan?" Super-Genius Jules called after him.

"A really, really *dumb* plan," Jules said over his shoulder as he climbed into his car and began backing down the driveway. "But it's the only plan I got, and I ain't tellin' you, 'cause I don't wanna hear you tellin' me what a damn *idiot* I am!"

Jules tuned his ex-cab's special radio to the police band. Listening in, he was able to determine that Slamazon had fled the scene of the NOPD Headquarters on South Broad Street and was heading south. A few minutes later, reports put her on South Carrollton Avenue.

"Oh my gosh," Jules said, "I know *exactly* where she's headin'. She's headin' for the Notre Dame Seminary, I just *know* it! 'Cause the seminary is full of men studyin' to be priests, members of the 'rotten, suppressive male higher-archy,' as she'd put it."

Sure enough, moments later, he spotted her on South Carrollton Avenue. She was running at an astounding speed, at least thirty-five miles per hour. He had difficulty keeping her in sight, but he didn't worry about losing her, because he knew precisely where she was going.

His plan had worked with his mother. Or at least it had contributed to Edna's return to sanity from evilness (unless her ingestion of the fumes of Super-Genius Jules's formula from Jules's formula-soaked shirt had done the entire trick). Still, Jules remembered the three of them, his mother, Jules, and Maureen, all singing that special song in rough harmony with the radio back in the good ol' days of the 1930s, when he'd had a waist size of only thirty-six inches. Nothing brought back memories like music, he knew. So hearing Jeanette MacDonald's and Nelson Eddy's "Indian Love Call" should, at minimum, soften Slamazon's hatred of Jules. Maybe she wouldn't pulverize him. Maybe she'd even calm down...?

He parked the Cadillac in a Handicapped Parking spot on the grounds of the Notre Dame Seminary. He didn't have any choice — all the other spots were filled, and Slamazon/Maureen was already smashing in doors, searching for seminary students and priests. "Come out!" she bellowed. "Come out of your hiding places, you Catholic male oppressors of gullible women!"

Jules ran toward her, despite her murderous fury, heedless of his own safety.

"When I'm calling you, ooo-ooo-ooo, ooo-ooo-ooo..."

Her face turned livid. "*Jules!*" As soon as he was within reach of her muscular arms, she back-handed him into a brick wall.

His head smacked hard into the wall. *Really* hard. As he plunged into the shadows, before he lost consciousness, he saw TV crews arrive in their mobile vans, the cameramen staying a respectful distance away from the rampaging Amazon.

"I am *SLAMAZON!*" she shouted at the cameras. "Matter Master, I declare you are a coward! A male worm who crawls on his white belly through the mud! I *dare* you to come face me!"

And then Jules heard no more, because he was out cold.

Hiro Matsuba could barely believe his luck. His primary quarry was calling him out on television? A challenge which was being broadcast on all four local news stations? A reckless challenge which revealed exactly where she was? He did not understand the reasoning for her strange transformation into a comic book villainess, Slamazon, but no matter — he would capture her and ensure she was dismantled even if she disguised herself as Ghidorah, the Three-Headed Monster.

The front portion of the Notre Dame Seminary was a scene of complete chaos, choked with overturned police cars, battered, bruised, unconscious police officers, and swarms of television camera crews. He parked across the street from the seminary, in the parking lot of a restaurant and bar called Ye Olde College Inn. He then trotted across the street to collect his quarry.

"Ho, Maureen Remoulade!" he called to her when he was fifty feet distant from her ongoing rampage. "Matter Master is here to accept your challenge, woman!"

Slamazon/Maureen put down the sofa from one of the priest's apartments which she had been smashing to splinters. "Do not call me by that slave name!" she bellowed at him. "Now and forevermore, I am *SLAMAZON!*"

"Whatever you care to call yourself, body thief, I am here to rub your nose in the dust, thoroughly defeat you, and bring you back to the compound of the High Krewe, where your purloined body parts will be returned to their rightful owners."

Slamazon/Maureen did not grant Matter Master a verbal response. Instead, she uttered a fierce, animalistic cry of fury and charged him.

Matter Master used the two seconds it took her to reach him to transform his outer skin into titanium. Just in the nick of time — his skin changed at the very instant her fist struck him. Had she struck him with that same blow when his outer skin was no more than flesh, her fist would have cracked his sternum and ribs, compressed his heart, and likely killed him. As things stood, however, she screamed with pain and frustration when her fist struck one of the most impenetrable metals known to mankind or womankind.

"*Aaahhwww!*" she cried, rubbing her bruised fist. "What sort of sorcery is *this?*"

"No sorcery, woman," Matter Master replied. "Merely the results of a most beneficial mutation, plus a thousand years of Japanese martial tradition!"

"I don't need to *strike* you with my *fists* to *hurt* you," Maureen/Slamazon said. With that, she grabbed Matter Master's titanium-coated legs and used him like a club, smashing down the brick walls of the priests' dormitory (which, thankfully, had been evacuated as soon as the fanatical Amazon had begun her rampage on the grounds). She beat his upper torso against the brick walls unmercifully.

Matsuba fretted that, although his skin was titanium and essentially unbreakable, his brain remained vulnerable flesh — and if it struck the inner walls of his skull with enough momentum and force enough times, he could end up with a concussion. Also, all this was being captured on American TV — quite humiliating.

He struggled to free one leg from Slamazon's grip. It was difficult, but he somehow managed. Then, his boot filled with titanium, he kicked her in the nose with all his strength.

Slamazon dropped him immediately. "Yoo male pygmy — yoo bwoke my *nose!*"

Matsuba leaped to his feet. He was not quite as agile when coated with titanium armor as he was in his normal form, but he still managed to put his martial arts training to good use. While his opponent was tweaking her broken nose to determine the extent of the damage, he backed up, then ran straight at her and delivered a flying judo kick to her midsection. The combination of his increased mass and the hardness of his foot did what probably no other man on Earth could accomplish — knocked her flat on her back. Then, before she could protect her head and face, he kicked the side of her head six times with enormous force, until he saw her eyes turn up in her head and she lost consciousness.

Breathing hard, he spoke to his downed opponent in Japanese: "<You — you and Cutie-Scary Man... such fools... to think you could overcome a foe such as me with mere brute strength! Now you will pay for your foolishness, woman, as my fellow meta-human from Japan paid for his.>"

In a flash of green energy, he restored himself to his normal form. Then he knelt down to touch the unconscious Slamazon with his right hand. His touch produced an unexpected double effect — Slamazon turned back into normal Maureen Remoulade before immediately changing, at Matter Master's instigation, into a jointed plastic mannequin version of herself.

Waving at the incredulous TV cameramen and reporters, he carried the mannequin back to his car across the street. He did not care when the news reporters followed him at a distance; if any of them noted down or photographed his license plate number, it would not matter, for his cargo van was a rental.

He did not know, nor could he even suspect, that his other prime quarry, Jules Duchon, had lain unconscious a mere fifty feet or so from the site of the brief battle.

Matsuba returned to the High Krewe's compound. No squad cars had pursued him; most of the police cars in the Carrollton and police headquarters area had been totaled during Slamazon's rampage.

He carried the mannequin into the central house. Hecht and Otranto greeted him. "Call forth Besthoff-*san,*" Matsuba said. "Tell him I have captured Maureen Remoulade. Tell him I am now able to restore his three women."

A moment later, Besthoff appeared. He clapped his hands together with glee when he saw what Matter Master held in his arms. "Brilliant!" he said. "A masterpiece of planning! You have rendered her helpless *and* capable of being easily dismantled, all in one fell swoop!"

Besthoff led Matsuba to the inner chamber which held the coffins containing the comatose forms of Victoria (legless), Alexandra (armless), and Tula Ann (the worst off of the three — merely a head, two arms, and two legs lacking a torso). Matsuba turned to Hecht. "Would it be possible for you to bring me an adjustable wrench?" he said.

"Of course, sir," Hecht said and raced off to find the tool.

After Hecht's return with a wrench, Matsuba spent ten minutes disassembling the mannequin. He handed Besthoff the plastic head. "I'll use this as a focal point for the mantlepiece in the library," Besthoff said happily.

Matsuba took the plastic torso and placed it in the center of the coffin which held the various comatose but undead parts of Tula Ann. He arranged the head on the plastic neck, the arms at the plastic shoulders, and the legs beneath the plastic hips. Then he touched the plastic torso with his right hand. Green energy arced from his fingertips into the mass of flesh-colored plastic. What had been flesh-colored became real flesh... real *vampiress* flesh. Matsuba had been informed that when touching each other, a vampire's severed pieces would reunite.

This proved to be the truth. A body which had been a mass of parts was suddenly whole, a single form.

After half a moment, Tula Ann's chest began to rise and fall, as she began breathing again for the first time in three years (vampires did not need to breathe, but they did so out of habit). A moment later, her eyes fluttered open.

Besthoff took her hand. "Welcome back to the land of the undead, my dear, *dear* Tula Ann," he said.

Before another four minutes had passed, Matsuba had similarly restored Alexandra and Victoria.

"You are worth every penny we are spending on you," Besthoff said to Matter Master. "No other being on earth could have accomplished what you have." He kissed each of the restored women on their bloodless, pale lips and gathered them to him. "Now," he said, "the only item missing from our library's furnishings is Jules Duchon."

"And with all of his friends and family in our hands," Matsuba said, "he will have no choice but to come to us."

Fifteen

OHHH, *my achin' head,* Jules thought as he slowly returned to consciousness. Maureen, in Slamazon form, had certainly lived up to her temporary name — she had practically slammed the *shit* out of him. Only the return of his vampiric powers, which included a greater-than-mortal toughness and a quick-healing ability, had kept him from being far more seriously injured.

He heard voices around him, and people digging through stuff. He forced his eyes to open. The men milling around were priests and seminary students, looking to see what they could salvage from the complete ruin Maureen had made of their humble living quarters.

One of the priests noticed Jules and walked quickly over to him. "Sir," he said, "are you all right? Do you require medical assistance? I could call an ambulance— "

"Uhh, I'll be okay, I guess," Jules said, trying not to look at the prominent crucifix the priest wore around his neck. The priest offered his hand to help Jules up from the cracked pavement. Jules waved his hand away, not knowing whether his hand might burst into flames upon contact with the consecrated holy man. "You'd better not, padre," Jules said. "I'm over three hundred pounds. You could throw your back out tryin' to help me up."

He got up on his own. "Did you see what happened here?" he asked the priest. "Do you know where that great big woman who was messin' everything up went?"

"We were evacuated into the main building and barricaded ourselves inside while the mayhem was going on," the priest said. "I heard there was a battle of some sort."

Jules didn't like the sound of that... the father could be referring to his own short-lived contretemps with Maureen, or he could be referring to (Jules didn't even want to think it) Matter Master mixing it up with Maureen. "Where's the closest TV, father? I got me a need to find out what just happened here."

"There's a bar across the street," the priest said, pointing at Ye Olde College Inn. "They have a large screen television there."

"Thanks, padre. I owe you one." In that instant, Jules wished it were still possible for him to attend mass. This priest seemed like a good, down-to-earth guy, especially if he was familiar with the TV set at Ye Olde College Inn. He probably crossed the street pretty regularly to have a beer and watch the games with the neighborhood characters. Most likely, he gave a great sermon. With jokes, even.

Jules crossed South Carrollton Avenue, glancing up briefly to appreciate the hardy live oak trees which had survived Hurricane Antonia's winds five months earlier. He entered the bar portion of Ye Olde College Inn. Sure enough, the TV was playing a special off-hours edition of the TV news. He waddled over to the bar, his attention fixated on scenes of Maureen's recent rampage.

"What can I get for you, friend?" the bartender asked.

Jules almost asked for a beer, but then he remembered how violently his system had rejected the last Bud Light he had tried downing. "You got any fresh coffee?"

"Don't know how fresh it is, but we got some in a pot in the back. You wanna take a chance on it? Maybe it'll be okay if you doctor it up with enough creme and sugar? Tell you what — if it's lousy, I won't charge you."

"Fair enough," Jules said. "I'll just take it black — no need to bring out any creme or sweetener. Hey, did you see what went on across the street at the seminary?"

"Some of it. Me and the customers all went outside when that big lady started yelling stuff and smashing things up. But then a couple of cops told us to go back inside before they ran across the street to try to rein her in. So I missed everything else. But I've seen it all on the TV. Fox News is playin' it on continuous loop, practically. Just keep watchin', and you'll see the whole thing." The bartender went to fetch the cup of coffee.

Jules watched the coverage. When the scenes of Slamazon/Maureen beating up the cops ended, the newscaster came on and talked some about how mysterious it had been that such a powerful super-being, one who claimed to be a villainess straight out of a comic book, had shown up, first at the NOPD Headquarters on South Broad, and then at the Notre Dame Seminary. Then he said even more astounding footage would follow.

Jules watched with a sinking heart the arrival of Matter Master and his acceptance of Slamazon's challenge. He winced when he saw Matter Master break Maureen's nose. Fury boiled in his chest when he saw the Japanese assassin brutally kick Jules's wife in the side of her head, five times, until Maureen was knocked out.

But the worst of all was watching Matter Master transform the love of Jules's life, a woman he would sacrifice his own existence for, into a lifeless plastic mannequin.

He squeezed the edge of the bar so tightly that the polished teak fractured, then crumbled in his hand.

The bartender returned. "Here's your cup of coffee, friend. You're in luck — Sylvia in the back had just made a fresh pot." He noticed the damage to the edge of the bar. "Holy mackerel — how the devil did *that* happen? How could I have avoided seein' it? Was that busted up like that when you sat down?"

"Yeah," Jules said.

"Well, here's your coffee."

"Keep it." Jules put three dollars down on the bar.

"You want me to put it in a Styrofoam go-cup for you?"

"Don't bother; I lost my appetite," Jules said. "Gotta go. Got me a mission. Got an appointment to keep with a son of a bitch named Hiro Matsuba."

It had been a little over three years since the last time Jules had seen or spoken with Tiny Idaho, the anarchist who supplied him with weapons. Years and years ago, he'd chanced upon Tiny Idaho's little shop in a run-down strip mall in suburban Kenner when he'd taken a fare out to the 'burbs (and drained the fare's blood before dumping his body in the swampy part of Lake Pontchartrain to the west of Kenner). Tiny Idaho had operated a comic book store back then, not a pawn shop: Readwood Used Books and Comix. But it turned out Tiny Idaho had a bunch of "special merchandise" in a back room. Weapons — guns, explosives, crossbows... enough stuff to overthrow a small Central American republic, it looked like.

Jules hadn't bought any weapons from him on that first meeting; instead, he'd bought laughing gas canisters and a set of plans for installing them with a remote on-switch in his cab. Then Jules had installed an airtight plastic shield between the front and back seats of his cab, and he'd been all set to knock out fares in an easy and humane way, rendering them unconscious before sucking out all their blood and shooting them in the head (to make sure none would rise as vampires to contest Jules's food supply).

The very last time he'd seen Tiny Idaho, it had been to buy a special crossbow that would fire wooden-tipped arrows and garlic pellets. He'd used it in his war against Malice X. Tiny Idaho had modified the crossbow for him in a just a couple of nights. He was a good man, if a bit of a kook. Best of all, being an anarchist, he didn't bother with background check forms, so Jules knew he could buy as many guns as he needed with no questions asked.

He already owned one. He needed two more.

Jules pulled into the crummy strip mall which housed Tiny Idaho's ex-comix shop, now a pawn shop (which, as he saw from the big cardboard cutout of Batman in the window, still sold comics, too). He saw that Tiny Idaho had moved from the run-down strip mall's second floor to the first floor; his shop now occupied the space formerly occupied by the Lounge Lizard Bar. Jules had already given the little anarchist a call to tell him he was coming. Tiny Idaho was the only pawn shop owner in the whole metropolitan area who would bother re-opening this late at night for a special customer.

Jules accidentally drove over a deep pothole. The jarring impact made his passenger side door fall off again. Jules had done a journeyman's repair on it before his drive out to Kenner, figuring a cop would pull him over and maybe confiscate his car if he saw Jules driving a vehicle missing a door.

He stared out the gaping opening in his Cadillac at the door lying on the broken asphalt. "Aww, fuck it," he muttered. "Guess I'll bum-rig it again after I deal with Tiny Idaho." He had duct tape in his trunk, and his hands, with the return of his vampiric powers, were again powerful enough to re-bend the broken hinges. Or maybe Tiny Idaho would have a welding iron.

He parked, then rang the buzzer next to the front door. Tiny Idaho answered. He really wasn't *that* tiny; five-foot-four-inches, but with broad shoulders and powerfully built (especially for a guy in late middle-age). His red and gray beard still reached to his oversized Johnny Reb belt buckle, and his smallish eyes still appeared *huge* behind his thick bifocals. He was wearing a tee-shirt with the Super Friends on it, cartoon images of Superman, Batman, Wonder Woman, and Aquaman from the 1970s.

"Big Jules!" he said, vigorously shaking Jules's hand. "Been a few years, hasn't it?" He gave his customer a quizzical look. "Say, you aren't so big anymore. I'd say you've lost a hundred and fifty pounds since the last time I saw you! Am I right around the mark?"

"A hundred and eighty," Jules said.

"Wow, man! What's your secret? If it's some kinda diet powder, I'll sell it in the store — it's practically a miracle product."

"Afraid I can't say how I lost all this weight."

"Oh? Trade secret? I get it, man. You come up with something that lets you lose a hundred and eighty pounds and *keep* it off, the government'll wanna tax you forty percent — *sixty* percent if you include state and local. Me, I've always kept two sets of books — one for Uncle Sam, and one for me. Well, c'mon inside, Big Jules! What can I do you for this time? You need yourself another souped-up crossbow?"

"Not this time," Jules said. *This time, I ain't fightin' no vampire,* he thought. Matter Master would laugh at wooden crossbow shafts and garlic pellets. "Naww... this time, I'm goin' conventional. I need me a pair of pistols."

Tiny Idaho stepped behind his locked glass counter, which housed pistols of every type. "Mind if I ask what you'll be using them for? Home defense? Personal defense? Need something you can keep in the glove compartment of that cab of yours?"

"I ain't drivin' no cab anymore," Jules said. "This is a vendetta. Some son of a fuckin' bitch killed my wife, my mother, and my step-dad."

"Holy *shit,* man. That's *heavy-duty.*"

"You're tellin' me." Jules suddenly thought of something; Tiny Idaho might have the solution to the problem of Matter Master's metal skin. "Hey, this guy I'm gunnin' for, he wears body armor, like, practically all the time. You got anything that fires armor-piercing ammo?"

Tiny Idaho thought for a moment. Then his eyes opened even wider. "Yeah, man! I've got just the thing! It's a Russian sniper's rifle. It fires armor-piercing bullets, strong enough to go through the skin of a Humvee. You wanna see it?"

"Sure thing," Jules said.

He ended up buying the sniper rifle, a box of armor-piercing bullets, and a 9mm Beretta with a box of ammo for it. "You know of any late-night shootin' ranges around here?"

"There's George Shultz's place. He caters to the midnight Second Amendment enthusiast. Let me get you the address off the computer. He's over in Mandeville, on the other side of the lake, so it'll be a bit of a drive."

"That's all right," Jules said. "I got all night. I'm rusty. Gotta practice some before I head off on this vendetta. I ain't fired no gun — not any gun that's not stuck right up against somebody's head, anyways — since World War Two."

Tiny Idaho laughed, showing his tobacco-yellowed teeth. "World War Two! Yeah, right! Pull the other leg, Big Jules — you mean the Gulf War, don't you?"

"Yeah, the Gulf War, that was it. Doesn't really matter though. As President Grant said once, all war is hell."

Jules bum-fixed his passenger side door, bending the hinges together and using very liberal amounts of duct tape. He stuck his new guns in his back seat, then drove across the Causeway, which took him to the north shore of Lake Pontchartrain. The longest continuous bridge in the world... twenty-four miles long, and not destroyed or even seriously damaged by Hurricane Antonia, so it had been built right.

The North Shore had taken much less of a hit from the hurricane than the South Shore had. Driving through Mandeville, he hardly saw any damaged structures at all. Everything appeared back to normal. He spotted a twenty-four hour GoodiesMart (the 'burbs were good for *something)*, so he stopped in to buy three identical sets of casual clothing for a trio of ten-year-old boys. Then he continued on the route which Tiny Idaho had printed out for him, the route which would take him to the North Shore Shooters' Paradise Shooting Range.

The place wasn't much in the way of a paradise, but Jules figured it was good enough. He chose the easiest lane, the one where the target was only ten yards away. He told himself he didn't have to be a marksman, because he was planning on relying on the power of surprise. He put on a pair of sound mufflers and fired off half his box of 9mm ammo from the Beretta, then half his box of armor-piercing bullets from the sniper's rifle. His first shots from the Beretta went wild because he hadn't prepared himself for the force of the discharge and he only held the gun with one hand. He did better with the rifle, because it fit snugly into his fat shoulder and he hardly felt the recoil at all. The armor-piercing ammo made the paper target and the wooden barrier behind it explode into shreds and splinters.

Once he felt confident enough in his marksmanship, he drove over to an isolated lakefront park, far from any apartments or houses. He carefully checked out his surroundings to make sure there weren't any teenagers drinking or screwing nearby. Then he stripped off all his clothes.

"No fat midgets this time," he told himself. He had planned to pursue a variant of his successful strategy against Malice X, but he wasn't certain he remembered how to split into multiple bodies, like Doodlebug had taught him to do more than three years ago. Sure, he'd split into two bodies only three months ago, but that had been Super-Jules's superbrain guiding the transformation. Now he only had his standard brain to count on — or his *sub*-standard brain, as Super-Genius Jules would put it. "You can do it, Jules," he told himself. "No midgets, no midgets. No goddamn trio of midgets. This time, I've only got three hundred and twenty pounds to play with, not four-fifty. So each of my three bodies is only gonna be one hundred and seven pounds or so. That means I gotta transform into a trio of me at ten years old."

He closed his eyes and concentrated as hard as he could. It wasn't easy; there were owls out here in the woods. But then he thought of Maureen, thought of what Matter Master had done to her, what Matter Master had done to his entire family and most of his friends, and his concentration returned.

He had to make sure he kept all his mass, all his three hundred and twenty pounds, right here in the park. Usually when he did a transformation, into a bat or a wolf, he pushed the greater part of his mass (with a bat, nearly all of it) through the null dimension and into the bottom of his coffin, where it rested as semi-liquid proto-mass until he called it back again. But this time, he couldn't afford to lose even a pound to the null dimension and his coffin, not if he wanted his ten-year-old triplets to still be big enough to handle a pistol or a sniper's rifle. He figured a hundred and seven pounds wasn't too small; he remembered reading about Russian lady snipers at Stalingrad in World War Two, and he bet a bunch of them hadn't weighed much over a hundred pounds.

"A trio of ten-year-olds, a trio of ten-year-olds," he chanted to himself. He concentrated on an old photo of himself from 1900 or thereabouts, when he'd been right around ten and was dressed in a little sailor suit his mother had loved. His body began to quiver and smoke. He smelled his own bodily odors all around him. He felt the pull of the null dimension, the pull of his coffin, the pull of nearly a century's worth of habit. But he struggled against it, and he succeeded in keeping his mass (and all of his ass) right where it was.

The clouds of Jules-stuff split into three small clouds, each of an identical size. Then they resolved themselves into three chubby but handsome identical ten-year-olds, each around four-foot-six and one hundred and seven pounds. They looked like buck-naked triplets about to take a bath.

"Okay, I managed to do it once," Little Jules Number One said. The night was cool; he shivered. He also noticed how high and reedy his voice sounded. "Now let me do it enough times that it gets to be second nature," Little Jules Number Two said. "Matter Master ain't gonna stand around and let me fiddle with myself until I get it right," Little Jules Number Three said.

He changed back into a single, three hundred and twenty pound Jules. Then he transformed into three identical ten-year-old triplets again. He repeated this process five times, until he felt completely comfortable doing it and confident that he could do it at a moment's notice, even under great stress.

"Might as well try on those clothes I bought," Little Jules Number One said.

"Striped button-down shirt and jeans," Little Jules Number Two said; "no sailor suit this time." He noticed that he seemed to share thoughts with Jules Number One and Jules Number Three.

"Guys, I'll go get the bag of clothes out of the car," Little Jules Number Three said.

Little Jules Number One and Jules Number Two waited for Little Jules Number Three to come back with the clothes. Little Jules Number One checked out Little Jules Number Two's body. No hair under the arms; no hair to speak of on the chest; no hair around the dick, which was partially shielded by a small roll of pudgy fat. Even as a little kid, he remembered, he had tended towards huskiness. He felt his own chin. Not even a trace of beard stubble. Just a tiny line of peach fuzz atop his upper lip.

The three Juleses tried on their identical sets of clothes. The underwear, size 12-14, was a little on the tight side (they realized their progenitor should've bought boxers, not briefs), but the pairs of jeans (in a husky size) and the shirts fit well. The sneakers were one size too big, but the

Little Juleses figured they could always stuff newspaper into the toes of their shoes if they had to.

They wished they could go back to the North Shore Shooters' Paradise Shooting Range as the triplets and practice firing the pistol and the sniper's rifle at their smaller size and weight. But the minimum age to handle weapons at the shooting range was sixteen, and although they were each a husky ten-year-old who could probably pass for twelve, there would be no way the three of them could pass for sixteen.

They would just have to make do and pray for the best. Like Big Jules always did.

The three Little Juleses stripped off their clothes and folded them and placed them back in the GoodiesMart bags. Then they concentrated on a single fat man, and seconds later, they were a single, large-size, middle-aged Jules. He put back on his clothes and drove back across the Causeway towards his hiding place in the underground garage in the French Quarter.

The long drive gave him plenty of time to think about the following night and what he needed to do.

* * * * *

The next night, at 9:07 P.M., Jules parked his damaged Cadillac on the far side of Metairie Road from the patch of woods which fronted the High Krewe's estate; he pulled onto the swale alongside Metairie Cemetery. As he had many times before, he mused about the irony that a whole colony of vampires should live less than a quarter mile from the biggest cemetery in New Orleans. Or maybe it wasn't ironic at all; the cemetery had been there before the High Krewe had built their complex in the mid-1800s. Maybe they had picked the spot because they had *wanted* to be next to a big cemetery.

He crept through the woods as carefully and silently as he could, carrying his bag of kids' clothes, two pistols, and ammunition, with his rifle slung over his shoulder. His whole plan depended on surprise. If he were lucky, he'd kill Matter Master with his first couple of shots. If he were less lucky, he'd have to sacrifice a body or two in order to blow the fucker away. If he weren't lucky at all... well, Jules didn't want to think about that.

He'd have to be extremely patient with the security cameras. He had a lot of stuff to get over that wall, in addition to himself. When he still had a bunch of trees between him and the cameras, he stripped naked, folded his clothes, and placed them in a plastic sack. He then hid the plastic sack in the crook of a low-lying tree. *Wishful thinking,* he told himself. *But it's a good idea to think about these clothes waitin' for me out here. It's a good idea to think I'll be walkin' out of the High Krewe's palace tonight alive... or at least undead.*

He moved slowly closer to the security cameras. He was glad this was a mostly moonless night; even if the cameras were infra-red, they wouldn't pick him up by his heat signature, because his body temperature matched the cool outside air, and the darkness would help mask the visual. He hid behind a large, thick-trunked tree and watched the cameras. Oddly enough, they weren't rotating like they usually did. They were all pointed in various directions, leaving large gaps between their fields of observation.

Well, whatever the reason they weren't fully working, that certainly made his task easier. He wouldn't have to wait until the cameras had rotated out of his range to toss his stuff over the wall; he'd just have to pick a spot where they couldn't see him.

Naked, he tossed the bag holding his children's clothing and ammunition boxes over the wall. Then he tossed each of the pistols separately, then the rifle. Then he transformed himself into a bat, unable to fly because of its plumpness, but well able to climb the wall with its claws.

Once inside the compound, he transformed himself back into his human form. Then he went one step further and changed into the three ten-year-old triplets. The three of them got dressed in the kids' clothes and collected the guns, which had scattered about the compound's inner grassy perimeter. Little Jules Number One and Little Jules Number Two armed themselves with pistols; Little Jules Number Three held the sniper's rifle. They'd go over to Straussman's room and get their blood-father-in-law to let them into the main house so they could search for Matter Master. If need be, one of them could change his body into mist, flow under the door, and open it from the inside, if Straussman didn't answer the knock.

But they got lucky. The three Little Juleses crept around the side of the main house, to where Straussman's quarters were. From Straussman's door, they could peer into the compound's courtyard with its fountain and bat statue.

They saw Matter Master smoking a cigar next to the fountain, acting as though he didn't have a care in the world. *And maybe he don't,* Little Jules Number Three thought, shouldering his rifle. *Maybe he looks so goddamn relaxed because nine-tenths of his job is done. He figures all he has to do now is wait for me to slink in here, beg for him to restore my friends and my family, and then change me into a mannequin or a big garbage can or whatever. Then he can collect his hefty fee from Besthoff, Krauss, and Katz and waltz happily back to Japan without a scratch on him. Least that's what he figures...*

Matter Master was relaxed. But Little Jules Number Three wasn't. He was shaking like a leaf in a storm. He had wanted to take out Matter Master with a single armor piercing round to the head, but his rifle's scope jerked around like a Mexican jumping bean.

Then he remembered something. Something really, really bad. When he'd been a kid and he'd gotten nervous, very nervous, he'd get the hiccups.

He hiccupped. Almost simultaneously, Little Jules Number One and Little Jules Number Two hiccupped, as well.

Matter Master looked in their direction. He spotted at least one of the three Little Juleses. He dropped his cigar into the fountain and headed swiftly towards them.

Big Jules's plan was screwed. So much for surprise. "Fire away, guys!" Little Jules Number Three yelled.

All three Little Juleses fired their weapons. All three Little Juleses were knocked off their feet by the recoil, their shots going wild.

Little Jules Number Three was the first to get back on his feet. He mentally prepared himself for an immediate pummeling from Matter Master's metal fist. But he saw that Matter Master was flat on his back, too. Had one of the bullets struck home and knocked him down?

He saw a flash of green energy. Matter Master transformed his outer skin into a suit of metal armor. Little Jules Number Three knew that now only his sniper's rifle with its armor-piercing bullets stood any chance of penetrating Matter Master's metal skin. "Move out of my way, you two!" he shouted at his twins. "Give me space to fire my rifle at him!"

But they didn't hear him. They were too busy firing their pistols at Matter Master. Little Jules Number Three heard bullets thud into the ground, ricochet off the stone fountain, and *ping! ping! ping!* off Matter Master's seemingly impenetrable skin.

"Get out of my way, you two idjits!" Little Jules Number Three screamed. "Your pistols are useless now! He's got metal skin!"

Matter Master slowly got up. Little Jules Number Three noticed his enemy was favoring his left shoulder; that must've been where one of the bullets had struck home. But the wound had been covered over by metal skin and was no longer bleeding.

The Japanese assassin began running towards the three Little Juleses. "Scatter, you guys!" Little Jules Number Three yelled. "Make him chase all three of us separately! So long as he's got that metal skin, he can't use his right hand to turn us into garbage!"

Little Jules Number Three fired his sniper's rifle. Right after the crack of the rifle's discharge, he heard a much louder *ping!* than he'd heard before. Then Matter Master cried out in pain. "What — what have you *done* to me? I am supposed to be virtually *invincible!*"

Had the bullet penetrated? No — it had bounced off like the others. But it had deeply dented Matter Master's chest. Maybe it had broken his sternum or breast bone? Whatever it had managed to do, it obviously hurt like hell.

He knew he held the only weapon capable of hurting Matter Master at all. That meant he had to stay out of the assassin's clutches. "Tackle him, you guys!" he called out to his two twins. He hated to do it, knowing they were in for a terrible pummeling, but he needed for them to buy him some time.

They did as he said, knocking their enemy off his feet. Little Jules Number Three reloaded his rifle. He ran toward the fountain with its tall grooved stone column and its platform holding a bat statue atop it. He would have to run right past Matter Master and the other two Little Juleses, now rolling on the ground.

When he got close to the battling trio, he paused, trying to see if he could shoot Matter Master at extremely close range. But the three of them were wrestling so fiercely and rolling about so wildly, it made it impossible for Little Jules Number Three to get a bead on Matter Master.

Matter Master picked up one of the Little Juleses and hurled him across the courtyard. Little Jules Number Three finally saw an opening. Standing only ten feet away from Matter Master, he aimed and fired.

The bullet didn't *ping!* this time. This time, it went *crunch!* Matter Master screamed even more loudly than before. Little Jules Number Three saw that his armor-piercing bullet had partially lodged in Matter Master's back, inches from his spine.

Matter Master turned to pursue his most dangerous opponent. Little Jules Number Three resumed his race to the fountain. He splashed through the water and reached the stone column, then began scampering up it, aided by the cracks in its surface, which gave him handholds and places to wedge the toes of his sneakers. Matter Master was so close now, reaching for his legs—

But the remaining Little Jules, either Number One or Number Two, bruised and battered, made a heroic effort and tackled Matter Master, toppling him into the fountain. This bought Little Jules Number Three enough time to reach the top of the column. He pushed aside the bat statue to make room for himself. It plunged downward and shattered on Matter Master's head, dazing him. But chunks of it hit the other Little Jules on his head and knocked him unconscious.

Little Jules Number Three grabbed this respite and hurriedly reloaded his rifle. He couldn't see all of Matter Master, because his enemy was still sprawled in the fountain and the platform Little Jules Number Three stood upon blocked his view. But he fired down at what he could see. He hit Matter Master in the buttocks — not a fatal wound by any means, but a painful one, to judge from his enemy's pained outcry. "I will *kill* you for this *indignity!*" Matter Master screamed. "I will flay you alive!"

Matter Master got to his feet. He must've begun hugging the column, because now Little Jules Number Three couldn't see him at all. He began reloading. But just as he chambered his next bullet, he saw a flash of green light below. Matter Master must've changed his skin back to flesh! That meant he could use his right hand again—

The column suddenly collapsed beneath Little Jules Number Three's insignificant weight. Matter Master had turned the column from stone into cardboard!

Little Jules Number Three had a long way to fall. He landed hard and hit his head, and the impact made the rifle fly out of his hands.

He lay dazed, trying desperately to clear his vision. He was so cockeyed now that he couldn't see where Matter Master was. But he saw a green flash off to his right. In all likelihood, that meant Matter Master had transformed his skin back into titanium armor.

He heard the approach of heavy footsteps. "I do not know who you children are," he heard Matter Master say, "nor how you got in here, nor your reasons for firing guns at me. But *you* in *particular* have angered me greatly. Now that I no longer need fear your strangely powerful rifle, I am going to take my time killing you and your identical brothers. I think the first thing I will do is tear your head off your shoulders. Then I will do the same to your brothers. Once the three of you are headless, I will transform your headless bodies into easy chairs and your decapitated heads into matching pillows— "

"I wouldn't even contemplate that, if I were you," a very familiar voice said.

Little Jules Number Three's vision finally cleared. There, standing not more than ten feet from Matter Master, was Super-Genius Jules, wearing some kind of bizarre backpack and holding a spray nozzle pointed directly at the Japanese assassin.

Sixteen

SUPER-GENIUS Jules pressed a button which turned on his spray nozzle. Something black and pungent and *very* hot poured out of the nozzle. Little Jules Number Three instantly recognized that smell. It was tar! Hot tar!

Matter Master immediately lifted his left hand to shield his eyes. But that was among the last movements he was able to make. Super-Genius Jules continued spraying him, concentrating on thoroughly coating Matter Master's right hand. As soon as that dangerous set of digits was entirely coated and made useless, Super-Genius Jules approached even closer and began coating each and every joint in Matter Master's titanium armor. Within seconds, Matter Master was transformed into an immobile black statue of himself.

The door to the main house burst open. Little Jules Number Three saw the Triumvirate emerge into the courtyard — lordly Besthoff, crafty little boy Krauss, and wizened old Katz. Then came the servants, Hecht and Otranto (but not Straussman), then an Asian woman who Jules had never seen before.

"He has defeated the Matter Master?!?" the Asian woman cried with disbelief. Little Jules Number Three saw her fangs — she was a vampire! She transformed into a white-furred wolf and charged at Super-Genius Jules. He sprayed the lawn just in front of her with hot tar, stopping her in her tracks.

"Wait!" Super-Genius Jules cried. "Before you attack me, I have a bargain to propose to Matter Master! You should listen closely, for my bargain means advantages for us all!"

The Asian woman had begun circling around Super-Genius Jules, looking for an opening to charge once more. "An Lai, halt your attack!" Besthoff commanded the white wolf. "I would hear this strange version of Jules Duchon out. He sounds far more intelligent than the standard version."

An Lai transformed herself back into a human woman, then quickly (and modestly) re-arranged her skirt and blouse, which had become disheveled during her transformation.

"Thank you, Georges Besthoff," Super-Genius Jules said. He then turned to Matter Master. "Hiro Matsuba, we are stalemated. You cannot move, because the joints of your armor are embedded with tar. But you also cannot transform back into human flesh, because the hot tar would sear that flesh and permanently burn eighty percent of your body; your face and hands would suffer the worst damage."

"What... what is your bargain?" Matter Master managed to gasp, moving his jaw with great difficulty.

"Wait just a minute!" Little Jules Number Three said. "Super-Genius Jules, if you're so damn *smart,* how come it took you the better part of a *week* to come up with this hot tar idea?"

Super-Genius Jules looked condescendingly at his ten-year-old version. "Oh, I came up with the *idea* immediately. It was the *implementation* which took me a week. I had to formulate a version of hot tar which could be projected at a distance through a sprayer, yet be compact enough to be carried in a steel bubble on my back. Then I had to formulate another compound which would immediately remove the tar."

"*Remove* it? Why the hell would you want to do *that?* He'll just attack again and turn you into a stupid orangutan, or maybe a statue of a stupid orangutan."

"That is where my bargain comes in," Super-Genius Jules said. "You interrupted me; allow me to continue." He picked up one of the discarded pistols, then turned to Matter Master. "Hiro Matsuba, do you understand that you are currently at my mercy? That if I wished to, I could approach you before any of your allies could stop me and place this pistol's muzzle inside your mouth, killing you by destroying your brain? The bullet would work its destruction most thoroughly, ricocheting inside your armored skull."

"I — I understand this," Matter Master said with difficulty.

"But I prefer not to pursue this course of action." He tossed the pistol aside. "My bargain? I will cleanse you of every speck of tar, so that you will feel comfortable returning to your standard form, with your ability to manipulate matter restored. In exchange, you will restore each of Jules's family and friends to their original forms. With the exception of Maureen."

"*Whaaaaat?*" Little Jules Number Three gasped. "You big-brained *bozo!* How could you possibly leave Maureen outta the bargain? Don't you love her just as much as I do?"

"Of *course* I do, Jules," Super-Genius Jules said. "Don't be an idiot. You haven't heard the rest of my bargain. If I insisted that Matsuba restored Maureen to her condition *ante la guerre* — before this war between you and the High Krewe got its start — the war would simply continue in another form. Perhaps not tonight, perhaps not tomorrow night, but on some night to come. They would hire other operatives to retrieve the stolen body parts once more. Also, whatever their past sins may have been, Alexandra, Victoria, and Tula Ann deserve to live out the rest of their undead lives. Yet so does Maureen."

"So how does your bargain fix that?" Little Jules Number Three said. "Either the High Krewe gals get the body parts, or Maureen does. It's not like they can share them— "

"*I* will become the new body for Maureen's head."

"*You?*"

"As part of our bargain, Matsuba will restore Maureen's head from plastic to flesh and bone, and under my guidance, he will transform my one hundred and eighty pounds of vampiric mass into a body upon which to place that head — a woman's body, of course."

"So you're gonna *sacrifice* yourself for Maureen?" Little Jules Number Three asked.

"Of *course*. Wouldn't you? Didn't you risk death by coming here to so injure Hiro Matsuba that you could then force him to restore Maureen and your other family and friends?"

Little Jules turned red with embarrassment. "Uhhh, actually, I just came here to *kill* him. I didn't think of none of that other stuff..."

"That is a perfect illustration of why *I* am a super-genius and *you* are barely above the moron level."

"Uhh, y'know, I'm three hundred and twenty pounds when I'm in my standard body," Little Jules Number Three said. "Maybe I'm not as *stupid* as you think I am, 'cause if I gave up half of that to Maureen, I could still be a hundred and sixty pound vampire... a little on the skinny and scrawny side, but certainly doable. Instead of you sacrificin' *all* of yourself, how about *me* sacrificin' *half* of myself? You deserve to have an undead existence, too, Super-Genius Jules... just like Maureen, Tula Ann, Victoria, and Alexandra. Just like *me*."

For the first time Jules could remember, Super-Genius Jules looked to be at a loss for words. This didn't last long, however. "I — I thank you, Jules. That is an offer worthy of the being who served as my progenitor. But the person to make the sacrifice must be me. There are two reasons for this. For one, Hiro Matsuba has not yet agreed to our bargain. He must realize by now that I am the most dangerous foe he has ever faced, the only being on Earth who could end his lucrative career as an assassin-for-hire any time I have a notion to do so. In getting rid of me, he rids himself of the only true danger to his continuing his present lifestyle;

indeed, to his own continuing existence. I said that this bargain must have benefits for us all. I will benefit in knowing Maureen will be restored. The Triumvirate benefits by having their three blood-daughters safely returned to them after a three-year absence. You benefit by having your wife, family, and friends returned to you; and incidentally, Maureen's body will no longer react to you with revulsion. Hiro Matsuba benefits by being released from his current imprisonment and by knowing that his most fearsome and capable foe will be taken off the board.

"And actually, for me, there is one further benefit, the other reason why it must be me who makes the sacrifice. I will give Maureen a great gift, even greater, perhaps, than the gift of granting her a new body for her head to rest upon. Knowing this, I can cease to exist, happily, a completely fulfilled man."

He turned back to Matter Master. "Hiro Matsuba, have you heard all that I have said?"

"I have heard all."

"Do you accept my bargain, in all its terms?"

"I do."

"Do you swear this, upon your honor of yourself and the honor of your warrior ancestors?"

"I do so swear, my finest opponent."

"Very well. I shall release you, and you shall do all that we have agreed you shall." Super-Genius Jules adjusted the switches on his spray nozzle. Then he completely sprayed Matter Master with an anti-tar solvent of his own formulation. The gooey black tar turned to a viscous black liquid and dripped away onto the lawn (unfortunately killing the grass, but the High Krewe could afford to re-sod the courtyard).

Matter Master experimentally moved his limbs. Little Jules Number Three saw that Super-Genius Jules's solvent had restored him to full mobility. Then, in a flash of green light, Matter Master transformed his titanium skin back into flesh, no longer risking fatal burns from the hot tar.

"Keel them now!" the desiccated Katz cried. "Welsh on your foolish bargain! Keel the Juleses!"

"No!" An Lai shouted. "No, Matsuba-*san,* you must not. As your employer, I forbid you to follow Mr. Katz's command. You listen to me, not him. You are a man of honor. You gave your word. You must abide by it."

"There is no need for you to tell me that," Matter Master said. "A man of honor does not need to be reminded of the requirements of honor."

"Glad we cleared that up," Little Jules Number Three said. "Before we go get everybody back to normal, I'd like to get back to normal myself." He shook both of his unconscious brothers until they were each awake once more. "C'mon, guys... it's time to make one Big Jules again." He turned to the assembled company. "Uhh, pardon us, everybody. We kinda gotta get naked now. Feel free not to stare."

Each of the Little Jules stripped off his clothes. Each closed his eyes and concentrated. Then each of them turned into a column of flesh-scented mist. The three columns merged, and a man-shaped figure quickly formed. A rather large, rotund man-shaped figure, quite familiar to everyone in the courtyard.

"Jules Duchon!" Besthoff said, astonished despite himself. "When I heard the Jules with the elongated head speaking to the little boy, I assumed the little boy had to be you. But I had no idea, I simply had *no idea* you have the ability to split yourself into multiple bodies and control all of them... most formidable!"

"He was never in control of me," Super-Genius Jules said, slightly affronted. "I am my own person, thank you, and I make my own decisions — intelligent, carefully considered decisions."

Jules remembered that his full-sized clothes were still hidden in a bag in a crook of a tree in the woods fronting the High Krewe's compound. Not wanting to walk around grossly naked, he grabbed one of the Little Jules's stretchy cotton-poly shirts and turned it upside down, stepping into its arm holes and using the shirt as an ill-fitting set of underwear.

An Lai stared with amazement at both Jules and Super-Genius Jules. "Which of you is my blood-father?" she asked them both.

"Blood-father?" Jules said. "What the heck are you talkin' about, lady? I ain't never seen you before... least, I don't think..."

"A vampire who looked exactly like you, only bigger and fatter, drove me in his cab from the French Quarter to New Orleans East nearly thirty years ago," An Lai said. "He then attacked me and drank my blood, then dumped me in a nearby swamp after shooting me in the head. But his aim was off; my brain was not destroyed. And the water was so murky that it protected me from the sunlight for the necessary three days and nights. I became a vampire myself. So which of you should I call my blood-father?"

"Both of us," Super-Genius Jules said. "Until three months ago, I had no separate existence. I was merely a part of the original Jules Duchon. Astounding as that may seem."

"I see," An Lai said. "Let me tell you *both* this, then. For nearly thirty years, I have *hated* my blood-father. He left me to rot in that swamp after having attempted to destroy my brain. Yet now I am confused... for with each of you offering to sacrifice yourselves for the life of your woman, I see a nobility in you, a sense of honor I would not have suspected. This night... this is the most perplexing night I have experienced since that night nearly thirty years ago when I first emerged from the waters and mud of the swamp, not knowing what I was, what I had become."

She bowed to them both. "I... I accept you *both* as my blood-fathers. I am... honored to have such noble ancestors."

A few minutes later, the company had reassembled in the library of the High Krewe. Jules looked around him with both a sense of wonder at the various objects which Matter Master had created and a sick feeling in the pit of his stomach that his family and friends had been forced to endure such transformations.

He saw a giant ball of yarn; that was most likely his mother. He saw a giant bottle of aspirin; that, given Matter Master's sick sense of humor, simply *had* to be Doc Landrieu. He saw a plastic mannequin which was the spitting image of Erato, complete with blood-stained clothes. He saw a six-foot-tall plush stuffed animal version of Hello, Kitty, which was most likely Shogo. He saw various pieces of brand new-looking furniture around the library, tables which hadn't been here the last time he'd seen this place. Any of those could be Doodlebug or Emiko.

And he saw Maureen's plastic head and neck, sitting on the library's mantlepiece like a trophy. Seeing that made his blood boil with fury, but he kept himself in check. Soon, very soon, thanks to the bravery, self-sacrifice, and super-brain of Super-Genius Jules, everything would be made right.

Matter Master approached the giant bottle of aspirin first. He touched it with his right hand, and the green energy with which Jules had become so familiar arced from Matsuba's fingers into the oversized plastic container. Suddenly, in a great flash of green light, Amos Landrieu reappeared.

"Where am I?" he said. Then he looked at Matter Master. "It's the assassin! But where's my gun?"

"Stand down, John Wayne," Jules said. He explained to Doc Landrieu all that had happened over the past few days. "Let's get Matter Master to restore Mom next. I'll let you do the explainin', this time."

Matter Master placed his right hand on the giant ball of knitting yarn, which measured five feet in diameter. After the green flash of light, a very bewildered Edna Dorothy Landrieu found herself standing in the middle of the High Krewe's library.

"Where in the name of Mary, Joseph, and Jesus *am* I?" she said.

"Wasn't I just tryin' to shoot some Jap?" She turned and saw Matter Master. "Oh my gosh — it's *him!*"

Amos Landrieu embraced his wife before she could begin screaming. "It's all right, dear," he said. "Jules explained everything. Everything's going to be all right now."

"How about you do poor Erato next?" Jules asked Matsuba.

Matsuba nodded. He approached the kneeling plastic mannequin and restored Jules's former best human friend.

Erato tried to rise. But he fell back to the ground, groaning.

Jules rushed over to him. "Easy there, Erato, easy. You've lost a *huge* amount of blood. It's gonna take your body a while to restore it all. See that guy over there, Hiro Matsuba?"

"You — you mean the *assassin?"* Erato gasped.

"Yeah, the big, bad assassin. I gotta let you know, pal, Matter Master saved your life by changin' you into a plastic mannequin when he did. That skank Pearl was just about to suck you dry, and if she had, you'd be a vampire now, like me. She tried capturin' Maureen, too, and I had to rescue her. Sorry to say, I wasn't in my right mind; otherwise, I woulda tried rescuin' you both. I'm sorry, Erato. But without meanin' to, Matter Master did the job I failed to do."

Rory "Doodlebug" Richelieu came next. When his eyes cleared from the green flash, he stared around the room in wonder. "I — I was a coffee table, wasn't I?" he said. "I vaguely remember a mug of blood resting on my surface, and Mr. Besthoff putting his feet up upon me."

"I will restore Johann Straussman next," Matsuba said, walking toward one of the library's end tables.

"No, you certainly will not!" Besthoff huffed. "Straussman is a traitor to the High Krewe. I absolutely *forbid* that he be restored!"

"Ahh, Mr. Besthoff?" An Lai said. "Did you read all of the contract which you and I signed? In a situation such as this, which requires arbitration, *I* am contractually assigned as the arbitrator. My blood-father's agreement with Matsuba-*san* stipulated that *all* of Jules's relatives and friends be restored or freed. That includes Mr. Straussman."

Besthoff began to protest, but he then thought better of it. Jules figured that a man as punctilious as he would die before breaking a contract he had signed, even if he hadn't read all the small print. "Very well," Besthoff said at last. "I must bow to your authority in this, An Lai. But I have stipulations of my own, stipulations to give to Straussman upon his return to the undead."

Matter Master restored Straussman. As soon as the butler regained his human shape, before he could say a word, Besthoff strode toward him and delivered two powerful slaps to Straussman's cheeks. The second blow was so strong that it knocked the newly restored vampire to the ground.

"Consider yourself *banished,* Johann Straussman. Although I am forced by An Lai to allow you your life back, she cannot force me to retain you within this household. You will exit this compound *immediately,* upon the conclusion of tonight's proceedings."

Straussman regained his footing, then bowed his head in silent submission. Doodlebug was the first to approach him. "Johann," he said, "you may not know me well, but your being Maureen's blood-father makes you my blood-great-grandfather. I owe you my undead existence, and I know you have been a good friend to both Jules and Maureen. Come with me to California— "

"Your precious paranormal and meditation institute is *closed,* Ms. Richelieu," Besthoff said. "You have invited our disgraced butler to share your destitution."

"Oh, I know that, Mr. Besthoff," Doodlebug said. "I am not so naive as to presume to beg you for mercy. I willingly take my punishment." He turned back to Straussman. "But Johann, my institute is worth rebuilding. Come help me raise funds. Be my partner. You have great skills in both poetry and music, and your centuries of being a butler have given you talents in hospitality which will make you an ideal host for our customers. I collect payment in both money and blood. You will share in both, equally with me."

Straussman eyed him warily. "You — you would do this for me, one who is a virtual stranger?"

Doodlebug smiled. "You're no stranger. You're my great-grandfather."

Straussman walked to stand by Doodlebug's side.

"Lastly, I will restore my fellow countryman, the Cutie-Scary Man," Matter Master then said.

"Hey, before you do that," Jules said, "you better let me get hold of his arms. Otherwise, he's gonna think he's still in a fight, and he's gonna jump all over your ass."

"That is wise," Matsuba said.

Jules walked over to the giant Hello, Kitty plush doll, stood behind it, grabbed its arms, and twisted them behind the doll's back. "Okay, I'm ready when you are," he said.

Matter Master performed his mutant magic upon the Hello, Kitty doll. Shogo returned, but as the same monstrous version of Hello, Kitty as he had worn when he had fought Matter Master several nights earlier.

"Where *is* he?" Shogo shouted. "I will tear him to *pieces!* I will bite through his jugular vein! I will sever that right hand of his of which he is so proud— "

"Whoa, Kitty, *whoa!"* Jules yelled from behind him, still holding his arms. "Our war with Matter Master is *over,* pal. Don't be like that Jap soldier on a desert island who fought World War Two for forty years, okay?"

Jules felt Shogo stop struggling. There was a green flash, and he returned at last to his human form. He stared harshly at Matter Master. "What have you done to my cousin, villain?"

"An Lai," Besthoff said, "I assume the bargain struck between the super-intelligent Jules Duchon and Matsuba means that we must release Anime Girl from her imprisonment?"

"Yes, it does," An Lai said.

"Hrmmm. All right, then — Hecht, go free Anime Girl from my old coffin, will you? She must be getting quite hungry and thirsty by now."

Hecht scampered toward the exit.

Super-Genius Jules, regular Jules, and Matter Master all looked at one another. Jules felt a lump in his chest. Now the only person left to restore was Maureen.

Seventeen

"IN what order shall this be done?" Matter Master asked Super-Genius Jules. "Shall I transmute you into a new body for Maureen Remoulade first, or shall I initially restore her head to flesh and bone?"

"I would like my final vision of things to be a vision of Maureen's face, restored," Super-Genius Jules said. "Restoring her head first, before you have prepared me as a body for her, will not hurt her. Remember, vampires do not need to breathe, even though they may prefer to do so out of old habit. She will be unable to speak, due to a lack of lungs with which to provide air to flow over the vocal cords in her neck, but her eyes and ears and brain will function just fine. Thus, she will witness my change and realize what I have sacrificed in order to restore her. Her gratitude is unnecessary; my best and sole reward will be the fleeting knowledge that my actions have been essential to restoring her to her full form and functionality. And I will give her something extra, besides, something only she will know. A *lagniappe* gift from me to her, a little something extra, in addition to the gift of a vampiress's body."

He approached Matter Master. "In order for me to guide you, I must transmit electromagnetic pulses directly from my brain into your brain. This is a form of telepathy, completely harmless to you. I can perform this feat over a short distance, but the transmission will be stronger and far more effective if we are in physical contact. Allow me to touch your head with my fingertips, and I will provide you with all the knowledge you need. But first, please do me the enormous kindness of restoring my beloved's head. Jules, go gather Maureen's head from the mantlepiece."

"Sure thing, S. G. Jules," Jules said. He walked to the mantlepiece, then reverently picked up the plastic mannequin head and neck of Maureen. *Looks like she comes straight from a department store's display window,* he thought.

He placed the plastic head and neck upon one of the library's reading tables, making sure to balance it on its neck so that when Maureen's eyes began functioning, she wouldn't be seeing the room sideways. He made sure to point her eyes at the place in the room where Matter Master first would receive Super-Genius Jules's transmission, and then would transform him into a new body for Maureen.

Super-Genius Jules took off his bulky backpack and placed it and the connected spray nozzle on the floor. "Doctor Landrieu," he said, "inside that back pack you will find a compartment which contains surgical thread and all the instruments you will need to attach Maureen's head to her new body. I have also procured a local anesthetic, in both cream form and injectable form, so that she will not experience any pain or discomfort whilst you are performing your operation."

Wow, that Super-Genius Jules really is a genius, Jules thought. *He's thought of everything. Makes me kinda proud that he was once a part of me.*

"Proceed, please, Hiro Matsuba," Super-Genius Jules said.

Matter Master approached the reading table and placed his right hand upon Maureen's plastic forehead. Green energy arced from his hand into her forehead, and the plastic head briefly glowed green. Then an undead pallor returned to those cheeks, no longer a pinkish-beige plastic. The blonde hair turned from nylon to strands of human hair.

Jules saw her eyes wildly scan the room before they settled on him. "Welcome back, honey!" he said. Then he saw her lips silently move. He was so accustomed to staring at her face, he found himself easily able to read her lips. "Where are you?" he said, repeating what she silently mouthed. "You're in the library of the High Krewe of Vlad Tepes. Why can't you — hey, wait a minute, could you repeat that, maybe? Why can't you talk or move your head? That's 'cause you don't have a body yet, honey. All you've got is a neck and a head. No, no — don't get all upset! Super-Genius Jules over there is gonna take care of everything. You'll see. Why is he touching Matter Master's head? Wait and see, babe, just wait and see..."

Jules saw his big-headed twin close his eyes and concentrate hard. His fingers touching Matsuba's head vibrated with strain. Matter Master had also closed his eyes, the better to listen to the telepathic message. Jules saw the Japanese assassin smile. "That is a fine gesture, my one-time foe," Matsuba said. "A delicate operation, but I am fully capable of fulfilling your wishes, now that you have transmitted to me all of the biological instructions. I shall be honored to carry forth your plan. I am only saddened that the world will now be without you, even though you are the most dangerous and skilled foe I have ever faced."

Super-Genius Jules broke contact, opened his eyes, and pulled over a straight-backed chair from one of the reading tables. He sat down, and Matter Master knelt beside him. Super-Genius Jules once more placed his left hand atop Matsuba's head, and this time Matter Master touched Super-Genius Jules's hip with his right hand.

Jules held his breath. The familiar green energy flowed from Matsuba's fingertips into Super-Genius Jules's hip, then scattered at light-speed throughout his body. Jules's big-brained twin began glowing an intense green, intense enough to light the entire library, intense enough to make Jules's eyes tear up looking at it. It was like staring into a green sun.

Super-Genius Jules's body began to shift shape. His great, tall head melted into his shoulders, which became narrower. His hips widened considerably, and his chest expanded with a voluptuous bosom. His thighs thickened, as did his calves, but in a most shapely way. Jules could tell that his former twin was becoming shorter as his one hundred and eighty pounds of mass were redistributed into the form of a zaftig, hourglass-shaped woman, minus her head.

At last, Maureen's soon-to-be new body stopped changing and stopped glowing. Jules certainly liked what he saw. He and Super-Genius Jules had obviously shared the same taste in women's shapes. He could hardly wait until Amos Landrieu carried out the final step. "Doc...?" he whispered hoarsely. "You think you could, uh, y'know...?"

Looking astonished at the transformation, Doc Landrieu walked over to Super-Genius Jules's bulky backpack, lying on the floor. He opened it and dug out a medical kit, complete with surgical stitchery and anesthetics. Then he began walking toward the reading table which held Maureen's head.

"Wait!" decrepit old Katz cried out, raising his liver-spotted hand in defiance. "Who said you could haf the head?"

"What are you talking about, you petrified old fossil?" Jules said. "Matter Master and Super-Genius Jules made a bargain— "

"That bargain stated that Matsuba would restore your family and friends to *their prior state,* did eet not? And vhat vas Maureen Remoulade's prior state? A severed head and neck! The bargain said *nuthink* about your having the head reattached to a body...

"So I claim the head!" Katz shouted triumphantly. "Eet looks so *good* on our mantlepiece! You can take the body and do with eet as you weesh, but the head ees *mine!*"

"That's complete *bullshit,* you hoity-toity old fuck!" Jules advanced menacingly on the ancient vampire, his hands stretched out to throttle him. "We're takin' Maureen's head, and we're gonna stick it on her new body, and in the meantime, I'm gonna stick my *fist* down your throat, after I squeeze it like a tomato can— "

"Wait!" Besthoff shouted. "There must be no further violence in this house. An Lai will decide. She is the arbiter. Do you concede her authority in this, Duchon? Or must we start our war all over again, this time with every vampire in this household arrayed against you?"

Jules still wanted to sock Katz in his ugly, wizened old face, but he lowered his fist. "I — I'll listen to whatever she decides. I trust her to do the right thing."

"The right thing is to end this now-senseless war between you and the High Krewe," An Lai said. "My decision? Your right to reattach Maureen's head to the new body which your twin, my other blood-father, made for her was implied in the original bargain, although not explicitly stated."

Katz pointed a bony finger at her in an accusing fashion. "She shows *favoritism!"* he whined.

"There is no favoritism in my decision," An Lai said firmly. "Only a sense of fairness, and a desire to see this conflict end. The three High Krewe young women have been restored. Maureen Remoulade has lost the body parts which were stolen on her behalf. It is only right that a Jules Duchon sacrificed himself to provide her with new body parts, donated, this time, rather than purloined."

Katz stomped out of the room in a semi-senile pique. Jules gestured for Doc Landrieu to resume what he had started. Amos set down the medical bag next to the headless female body which Matter Master and Super-Genius Jules had made, then walked quickly to the table which held Maureen's head. He picked it up most carefully and walked with it back to the body. "Jules," he said, "I need you to hold the head in place while I apply the anesthetics and sew it on. She'll have some scarring, just like she did last time, but she'll be able to cover it with a jeweled choker, if she wishes. Otherwise, I think she should be pleased with the results, for it is a *lovely* body."

"You're tellin' me," Jules said. He practically floated across the room to hold Maureen's head in place.

In five minutes, Doc Landrieu finished his work. Maureen was now able to speak.

"How come I'm so much *shorter* than I was before?" she said, looking down at herself. "And whose idea was it to give me breasts like giant cantaloupes and hips as broad as the beam of the battleship *Missouri?*"

She stared accusingly at Hiro Matsuba. But Jules, looking abashed, raised his hand. "Uhh, I guess that would've been *me,* hon. See, Super-Genius Jules and me, we had the same taste in women. You know what *I* like. Well, we both liked big, exaggerated hourglass shapes — pears with lots of curves up top. I guess he wanted to do me a favor, hon. I sure hope you don't mind..."

"*Mind...?*" Maureen looked as though she might explode. But then she exploded into laughter instead. "*Ha ha ha ha!* Oh, oh gosh, oh gosh — what *chutzpa* of me to complain, after all you all have done for me! This body's just fine! *Any* body would be just fine! I can't tell you how scared I was that the High Krewe would someday come and steal back my body. And now it's happened, but it's not awful, because I've got a *wonderful* new body. Thank you, Matter Master. You did *splendid* work. I only wish I could thank Super-Genius Jules somehow..."

"Hon," Jules said, smiling, "I think he knows how grateful you are."

"You know the first thing I need to do?"

"What? Have a big gulp of blood? I'm sure An Lai could convince Besthoff to be a gracious host— "

"No, that's not it," Maureen said. "I want to see Alexandra, Tula Ann, and Victoria, and both apologize to them and thank them. Mr. Besthoff, would that be possible? Are the girls strong enough yet to talk with me?"

"They have recovered very swiftly," Besthoff said. "I suppose it could be arranged."

A few minutes later, the trio of young vampiresses filed into the room. They all shuddered when they saw Jules. "Oh Varney," Alexandra said, biting her knuckles, "it's that *hideously* fat detective! I thought he was dead!"

"What's he doing here, Mr. Besthoff?" Victoria asked. "I thought you told us as soon as we'd been revived that he'd be a piece of furniture in the library by now. And who are all these *other* people? I sense that four of the other seven are vampires, but I've never seen them before..."

"Oh, you've seen *me* before," Maureen said. "You simply don't recognize me, both because it's been nearly a century since you saw me last and because I look so different now. I'm Maureen Remoulade. Victoria, I, uh, I sort of wore your legs for the last three years. These people are my friends and family."

"So *you're* the thief who stole my torso and left me a pile of arms and legs and a head?" Tula Ann said accusingly.

"You're the most horrible *monstress* I've ever encountered!" Alexandra said. "How could you; how *could* you...?"

"Please don't blame Maureen," Amos Landrieu interjected. "It wasn't her fault. She was dead, or in the netherworld, as you all put it, when *I* came up with the plan to utilize your body parts to make a new body for her resurrected head. You see, after she had been turned to dust by Malice X, much of the dust which had formed her body had blown away. Jules was only able to recover some of it. When Doodlebug over there recited his vampiric spell to resurrect her, the only part of her which was still whole was her head. The rest of her was a terrible mess, and I am told she howled with terrible pain, pain so unendurable that Doodlebug was forced to plunge another stake through her heart and send her back to the netherworld.

"I had recently been turned into a vampire myself by Malice X and his minions, and sensing that my old friend Edna Duchon had become a vampiress herself, I dug her up out of her grave in a consecrated graveyard and released her from the stasis which she'd endured for more than thirty years. I quickly fell in love with her, since we were now virtually the same age — during those thirty years, she had not aged, but I had — and I wanted to do something wonderful for her to prove my devotion.

"Her fondest wish, I quickly discovered, was that her son Jules should get married to a woman acceptable to Edna. I learned that you young vampiresses were on the hunt in downtown New Orleans, and I decided I could kill two birds with one stone — I could take several deadly predators off the streets, and I could make an ideal wife for Jules by combining the best parts of those lovely predators into a single vampiress, one who would be docile enough to follow our instructions.

"Originally, I placed a vampiress named Pearl's head atop Tula Ann's torso, Alexandra's arms, and Victoria's legs. But this Frankenstein's creation-like vampiress completely rejected Jules, was utterly repulsed by him, just like the man-made bride in James Whale's classic film *The Bride of Frankenstein.* Doodlebug, Johann Straussman and I then came up with the idea to resurrect Maureen's head and place it on the body instead of Pearl's head. Jules and Maureen were then married."

The three High Krewe young women screeched in unison. "Oh, *uuccch!*" Victoria said. "That's absolutely *revolting!*"

"Was — was the marriage ever *consummated?*" Tula Ann asked with dread in her voice.

"Yeah, I consummated it, all right," Jules said.

"Oh, I do believe I'm going to be ill," Alexandra said.

"I supposed he kissed my legs?" Victoria said. "I want to *vomit!*"

"*You* want to vomit?" Tula Ann said. "*I* had it the *worst* — I was the *torso!*"

"Girls, girls, just calm yourselves down," Maureen said. "Your parts' reactions were all driven by my brain, so you all had a fine old time, no matter what you may think of Jules now. Everything was working out just dandy until I drank too much of Kenji Tezuka's mutant blood, which gave me a *really* nice buzz, sort of a combination of liquor and pot. But it also gave the body parts of you three girls a form of independent willfulness, and you all began to express your revulsion of Jules in various ways. I went most of the last four months not being able to have conjugal relations with my husband— "

"Oh, poor you!" Victoria said sarcastically.

"Yes, 'poor me,'" Maureen said. "It was *terrible,* wanting to love my husband but being unable to so much as touch him with anything but my lips. But all that aside, I want to apologize to you girls for the three years you lost, and to thank you for the many months of life you were able to provide me with— "

"Wait a minute!" Tula Ann said, turning to Besthoff. "Mr. Besthoff, you didn't tell us it had been nearly *three years* that we suffered through this horror!"

"*Three years?"* Alexandra said, biting her knuckles again. "You mean for a whole three years minus four months, we had to endure that disgusting, obese creature slobbering all over us?"

"I did not want to overly stress you at the outset," Besthoff said. "I would have informed you of this eventually."

"Girls, Maureen said, "I've got something to share with you. Just in the past few minutes, I've found I'm able to look at things with a whole new perspective. I'd like to share that perspective with you." She briefly took each of the High Krewe's women's hands in her own hands in turn, showing honest affection and understanding. "Three years? Three little years? In the span of a vampire's potentially unending existence, three years are virtually nothing. They are three grains of sand on a beach a hundred miles long. They are three stars in a universe made up of a billion-billion stars."

Her face took on a beatific smile. "Rejoice, girls! Rejoice that fate has decreed that you live again, undead lives which need never end!"

Eighteen

JULES, Maureen, Amos, Edna, Doodlebug, Erato, Emiko, and Shogo walked to the front gate of the High Krewe's compound, only to find the gate had been broken down from the outside.

"What the heck happened?" Jules said.

"Oh, I believe I know," Maureen said, smiling a little smile.

"How would *you* know, hon? You were a plastic head when just about everything happened."

"Yes, I was a plastic head, Jules, but remember, my body used to be Super-Genius Jules. I retain many of his recent memories. I remember his battle with Matter Master. I also remember how he got into the compound. He knew the cameras had been knocked out by Emiko's entrance, and he could see they hadn't been repaired. Originally he had meant to sneak inside, but when he heard the gunshots from the courtyard, he figured that you'd jumped the gun, so to speak, Jules, and that you might need immediate assistance. So he just knocked the gate down and ran inside."

"Huh... good thing he did," Jules said. "That guy was a better friend to me than I ever knew. And here I spent the last three months figurin' him for a complete asshole." He turned to the rest of his friends and family. "Hey, y'all, you mind if you wait here for just a minute? I gotta go off into the woods and retrieve my clothing from where I left it. This little shirt definitely don't make a decent pair of underwear, and I'd kinda like to drive back into town lookin' more dignified than this."

"We must also go into the woods for a moment," Emiko said. "Shogo and I must retrieve the loyal *otaku* whom we hid in the crook of a tree."

The party reunited a few minutes later, with Jules now properly dressed and Shogo carrying the travel case which held the two *otakus* in their tiny coffin-like storage boxes. "Can I give everybody a ride back into town?" Jules asked. "I realize there're nine of us, but the Cadillac normally seats six, so Mom can sit on Amos's lap, and Emiko can sit on Shogo's lap, and, uh, Doodlebug could sit on Maureen's lap— "

"Actually," Amos said, "if it's all right with Edna, I think it would be very romantic for us to both change into bats and fly back to our home together. Are you up for it, dear?"

Edna hugged him tightly. "Smoochie-face, I'd fly to the *moon,* so long as you're next to me!"

"Jules, you'll take our clothes with you, won't you? We can grab them the next time we come over to work one of the tours."

"Sure thing, Doc," Jules said.

Just then, Erato moaned softly and began falling. Shogo was next to him and caught him before he hit the ground. "Uh, oh," Jules said. "Damn — he's lost more blood than I thought. Shogo, before I drop you and Emiko off at your hotel, I need to get my buddy here to University Hospital downtown so he can get a blood transfusion, pronto."

"No probrem, Jures-*san,*" Emiko said. "In fact, Shogo and I will call our own cab. That way Erato-*san* may lay on your back seat and be more comfortable on his ride to the hospital."

"Thanks, guys," Jules said, hugging both of his Japanese friends. "You make sure to come by Maureen's and my place before you head back to Japan, okay? We'll make a night of it and take in a set of jazz at Snug Harbor, plus *beignets* and coffee at Café du Monde."

Jules carried his dear old friend Erato to his Cadillac on the far side of Metairie Road and placed him gently in the back seat. Then he drove Erato, Doodlebug, and Maureen into town.

After taking Erato to the Emergency Room (the doctors directed that he be given an immediate blood transfusion, and then they recommended he be placed under medical observation for a couple of days; Jules blamed the injury on a wild animal in the swamps) and dropping Doodlebug off at his hotel, Jules found a lucky parking place directly in front of his and Maureen's home.

"What a find!" Jules crowed. "This night just keeps gettin' luckier and luckier!" He helped Maureen exit the car on his side, since her door was unopenable.

"Hon," she said, "let's not go inside yet. We haven't had an opportunity to do anything romantic for the past three months. I haven't even been able to hold your hand, not with Alexandra inside me putting up such a fight. What would you think about a nice romantic stroll along the riverfront?"

"Mrs. Duchon," Jules said with a toothy smile, "I think that's a capital idea."

This time, Jules didn't hesitate to hold Maureen's hand.

Their walk took them through Jackson Square. When they reached the edge of the wrought iron fence at the square's southwest corner, Jules noticed Maureen looking sad. "What's bumming you out, babe?" he asked. "I thought this little walk was gonna be special for both of us."

"Oh, it is, Jules. It *is*. But that's where Super-Genius Jules used to set his card table and tell people's fortunes. That's the last place I ever saw him."

"He'll always be a part of you, hon. Funny thing is, I always thought of you as a part of *me*. But now, in actuality, since Super-Genius Jules was originally a part of me, really *I'm* a part of *you,* ain't I?"

"The greater part, Jules. By far the greater part."

"Now that ain't so," Jules insisted. "If you're just talkin' *mass,* sure, I indirectly donated the biggest part of your body. But the most important part of you is up here," he said, gently touching her head with his forefinger. "*That's* the greater part of you, hon. If it wasn't, if total mass counted for more than your brain does, then during those more than three years you spent with them High Krewe gals as your body, you woulda adopted all their snooty, hoity-toity, rotten attitudes, wouldn't ya have?"

"I guess you're right, Jules," she said. But her voice was still tinged with sadness. "Let's keep walking to the river, shall we? I've got a feeling my mood will receive a big lift once we're there."

They crossed St. Peter Street and walked past the Jax Brewery restaurant complex toward Waldenburg Park, which fronted the Mississippi River. The fall air was clean, fresh, and invigorating; Jules felt a cool but not unpleasant breeze work its way down the collar of his shirt. He heard the sound of a distant calliope, as one of the excursion riverboats began its slow return to its dock.

Maureen stopped walking. Squeezing Jules's hand more tightly than he could ever remember her doing, she stared up at the stars for several lingering moments. Then her gaze took in the strings of lights illuminating the twin Crescent City Connection bridges to the west.

When she turned back to him, her eyes had filled with tears, but she was smiling an ecstatic smile. "Oh, Jules, the world, the sky, the very atmosphere which surrounds us... I never knew how *beautiful* they are... I simply never knew, never before tonight... You know, I used to miss the sun and the daylight terribly. But I'll never miss them again. Because I know I can spend an *eternity* staring up at those stars and never uncover all of their mysteries and wonder."

Jules couldn't remember his wife ever speaking in quite this way before. She sounded like Doodlebug... or maybe just a tiny bit like Super-

Genius Jules.

"Uhh, hon," he said, "this new, kinda poetical way you're talkin'... this wouldn't happen to have anything to do with that 'gift' Super-Genius Jules hinted that he'd give ya, does it?"

As her initial response, Maureen pulled Jules to her and kissed him. Then she held his face with both her hands and looked up into his eyes. "I've been debating whether or not to tell you this, Jules. I wouldn't want you to think of Super-Genius Jules as any sort of romantic rival. But, you know, he *did* love me, just as strongly as you do. Because he was a part of you, Jules."

"What are you tryin' to say, hon?"

"He *did* give me an extra gift, Jules, above and beyond the gift of a vampiress's body. I have... well, don't get all bugged out, but I now have a second brain."

"*Whaaaaat?"* Jules stumbled backwards, staggered by the bizarre notion.

"I *told* you not to get bugged out, Jules. See, this is why I was so hesitant to mention this. But I'm your wife, and you're my husband, and we shouldn't have any secrets between us. Yes, Super-Genius Jules gave me a second brain. A small auxiliary brain, located in my chest right next to my heart. He gave me not only his mass, Jules. He also gave me a part of his gigantic brain."

"Right next to yer heart, huh?" Jules scoffed. "What a romantic! He gives you an early valentine made outta brain matter!"

"Oh, Jules, my dear, dear Jules, *please* don't be obnoxious about this. *Please?"*

"Oh, okay, hon." There was no way he could say no to those gorgeous green eyes. "I'll be a good boy from now on, all right?"

"All right," she said. "It's just... oh, it's so hard to explain, Jules! All those things the nuns tried to teach me more than a century ago, all the mathematics and science and poetry — it all makes *sense* to me now! I can *understand it* now, even though I did my best to ignore my teachers all four years of high school! It somehow stayed in my head for more than a century. Oh, Jules, I want to learn more! I want to learn so much *more* than I know! I want to learn about every star we can see in the sky, and about all the planets and stars we can't see with our naked eyes. When I look at those lights adorning the bridges, I want to invent a way to make them even *brighter,* even more *beautiful.* Because *that's* our job as human beings, Jules — to fill a beautiful world with even *more* beauty, and I want to be a part of that!"

"Even though you're a vampire?" Jules asked shyly. He didn't quite know what to make of this new Maureen of his. "A predator who drinks other people's blood?"

"Aren't tigers predators, Jules? Aren't wolves? Aren't killer whales? Is there any way you can deny the *beauty* of all those predators, Jules? Is there any way you can deny that they all have a place in God's creation? And if *they* do, then *we* must, too. That's another thing I want to learn, Jules. I want to learn *our* place in the Creation."

Jules gulped. Hard. "And what about *me,* darlin'? What about dumb ol' me? You gonna get bored with me, just 'cause I can't do advanced math in my head, and I don't think tigers and killer whales are cuddly?"

"Oh, Jules Duchon!" she said, laughing. "Didn't I just say that *everything* has its place in the Creation? Doesn't *everything* include *you?* I'll bet I could spend a good chunk of my eternal life just pondering what makes you tick, you gorgeous hunk of man, you."

She again pulled him to her and kissed him. A long, lingering kiss under the crescent moon, at the edge of the Crescent City, atop the never-ending crescent curve of the world.

About the Author

ANDREW Fox has been a fan of science fiction and horror since he saw *Destroy All Monsters* at the drive-in theater at the age of three. His books include *Fat White Vampire Blues*, winner of the Ruthven Award for Best Vampire Fiction of 2003; *Bride of the Fat White Vampire*; *Fat White Vampire Otaku*; *Fire on Iron*, a Civil War dark fantasy; contemporary epic fantasy *The Bad Luck Spirits' Social Aid and Pleasure Club*; and *The Good Humor Man, or, Calorie 3501*, selected by Booklist as one of the Ten Best SF/Fantasy Novels of the Year for 2009. In 2006, he won the *Moment* Magazine-Karma Foundation Short Fiction Award. His stories have appeared in *Scifi.com* and *Nightmare.com*, and his essays have been published in *Moment* and *Tablet* Magazine. Companion volumes *Hazardous Imaginings*, a collection of his politically incorrect science fiction, and *Again, Hazardous Imaginings: More Politically Incorrect Science Fiction*, an international anthology which he edited, were published together in 2020. His next novel, *Hellfire and Damnation*, will be published in August 2021. He lives in Northern Virginia with his family, where he works for a federal law enforcement agency. He can be reached at http://www.fantasticalandrewfox.com.

CPSIA information can be obtained
at www.ICGtesting.com
Printed in the USA
FSHW022259031021
85204FS

9 781954 977990